DRAGON WITCH

DARK REALMS SERIES
BOOK 1

By
Kathy Kulig

Burnt Stilettos Press
EASTON, PENNSYLVANIA

Burnt Stilettos
Press

Kathy Kulig/Burnt Stilettos Press
kathy@kathykulig.com
www.burntstilettospress.com

Publisher's Note: This is a work of fiction. Names, characters, places, and incidents are a product of the author's imagination. Locales and public names are sometimes used for atmospheric purposes. Any resemblance to actual people, living or dead, or to businesses, companies, events, institutions, or locales is completely coincidental.

Dragon Witch/ Kathy Kulig. -- 1st ed.
ISBN 978-0-9903439-4-3

To those who dream in otherworlds

Contents

Space Drifter 1

Somerled 13

Dragon Tears 27

Needful Things 41

Water Spell 55

Green-eyed Dragon...65

Mating Ritual 73

Captured..83

Planetside Peril 91

Dragon Flame 95

GLOSSARY 108

ABOUT KATHY 111

A Note from the Author..113

Preview Edge of Passion 115

Preview Tattoo Witch 129

CHAPTER 1

Space Drifter

Brayden Stokes was seconds away from reaching across the table and grabbing Commander Krentz by the throat. Spotting the security guards across the common room, Brayden dug his fingers into the armrests and remained in his chair, knowing the three or four seconds of pleasure gained from choking his commander would not be worth it. Krentz had about eight years on Brayden and at least fifty pounds more muscle. The bald man who was his boss also stood a few inches taller than Brayden. Besides a court-martial, getting into a fight with Krentz would land Brayden in the infirmary for several weeks.

The commander lifted the new female recruit's legs over his lap and slid a hand up her skirt, then unfastened a couple buttons on her uniform shirt. Brayden watched the man stare at the exposed swell of her breasts. "You have such soft skin, Rhosyn," he said, his eyes half closed.

The woman leaned forward and smiled, not making any attempt to move away. Was it a forced or seductive smile? Brayden wasn't sure. Maybe she was too afraid to stand up to him. "Am I distracting you from your game, commander?" Rhosyn asked. A soft laugh rippled through her as if she teased him.

Brayden's muscles tensed, his fists clenched, but he knew the two guards drinking coffee and watching a video would be on him before Krentz struggled for a breath. And on the Outer Rim far from the Fleet's rules and regulations, it wasn't unusual for a commander to order a crazed crew member to take a one-way trip into the vacuum of space.

The commander unfastened yet another button on the woman's uniform shirt, exposing her nipples. She only giggled and wriggled her torso as she picked up her glass and sipped her drink. Realizing his chivalrous instincts were wasted on the woman, Brayden leaned back in his chair and let out a long breath. "We going to play this hand or are you going to play with your new recruit?" He was pushing his luck with his sarcasm, but they'd been together for ten years and Brayden could get away with some attitude especially when he was losing a hell of a lot of credits.

"I can handle both," Krentz said as he snaked his hand over his companion's shoulder. The woman twisted toward the groping Krentz, allowing for easier access. He then slipped his hand inside her open shirt and cupped her breast.

Gasping, she arched her back, apparently enjoying the attention.

Brayden averted his gaze. She'd signed on during the last stop at the Outer Rim Space Station and apparently hadn't wasted any time making her move on the commander. Figured.

"You're a fool, Brayden," Krentz said. "You can't possibly win and you can't bluff. The desperation is in your eyes. It's your tell."

"Maybe." Brayden held his ground. "You don't know what's at stake here." Taking a sip of his drink, Brayden focused his attention on his lousy hand of cards. Maybe Krentz's hand was worse, but he doubted it. Was the woman a setup to distract Brayden's game? Krentz had been known to pull that. Brayden knew what qualifications Krentz required of his recruits—at least from the women. A beautiful, intelligent and compliant crewmember on duty and in his bed. Her long, dark hair hung loose—not Fleet regulation for an officer, then neither was having her shirt unbuttoned down to her waist.

As she leaned over to glance at Krentz's hand of Robard's Bluff, every crew member in the room got a clear view of large round breasts and rosy nipples. Brayden's cock stirred despite his current problem—a hopeless and grave issue by the look of his hand. He was about to lose the final round and possibly his chance at getting his pilot's license back.

His jaw tightened at the consequences not only to his peace of mind but to innocent colonists desperate for survival. Krentz had already beaten two other crew members who were more interested in watching their commander fondle the new recruit than concentrate on the game.

"I'll raise you another credit," Brayden said as he tossed the gold chip into the pot, trying to bluff and maintain the confidence he didn't feel. He was screwed, he knew it, but he had to play the hand.

Krentz looked at the two crew members then at the pot of gold chips and chuckled. "Another month's worth of credits, eh, Brayden?"

"You don't get it, do you?" Brayden couldn't hide his anger, knowing he crossed a line with his commander with this tone. After all the transport jobs and all the colony settlements, the legal and illegal runs he did at the orders of Krentz, Brayden was still puzzled by him. He could understand working the system for financial gain, or higher rank. The farther out, the more corrupt the Fleet became. But Brayden didn't understand apathy for human life, and he couldn't respect the man for that reason.

Krentz raised his eyebrows. "Enlighten me." He poured himself another glass of Cahoon Jack and emptied the bottle. He held it up and gave the woman a look. "Would you, Rhosyn?"

She smiled. "My pleasure." Getting up, she rebuttoned her shirt, revealing a healthy amount of cleavage, and walked across the common room to the wall of storage compartments. With a tap of her finger a panel slid open and she selected a bottle.

Glancing over her shoulder, she apparently seemed satisfied that Krentz was still occupied with his cards. She stepped to another wall and switched on a computer monitor. Brayden wished the woman would finish what she was doing and fill Krentz's glass with the amber liquid. Getting the commander drunk was his only chance of winning. Brayden didn't dare drink another drop of CJ. He held the glass to his lips but didn't drink.

"Dammit, I'm responsible for those colonists on Krakatan. If you'd clear it with Fleet, I can get my license back and do a humanitarian run to rescue those people before their planet—"

Krentz slammed his fist on the table and the chips rattled. "I don't do favors unless there's something in it for me."

Taking a breath, Brayden focused his attention on his cards. If he didn't watch himself he'd never get his license back and he'd be stuck under Krentz's thumb for years while his ship, the *Zepar*, rusted in the docking bay.

Rapid keystrokes by the woman brought the computer screen to life. A series of numbers scrolled up but it was too far away for Brayden to see. She glanced over her shoulder and locked eyes with Brayden. Frowning, she shook her head. The monitor clicked off.

"Rhosyn, we're dry over here," Krentz groaned.

"Sorry, had a diagnostic to check."

"Good girl." Krentz pulled her close and kissed her when she sat back down, then undid the buttons on her shirt again. Brayden noticed the muscles tighten in Rhosyn's jaw, but other than that, she laughed and play-punched him in the arm. Yeah, Brayden really hated the bastard. "Beautiful, loyal, a good crew member and she knows how to suck cock."

Rhosyn playfully punched the Commander in the arm again and made a disapproving sound. "Sorry, darling, it's the CJ talking. Pour me a little more. Would you?" Krentz stroked her cheek gently, almost affectionately.

She filled his glass. Brayden didn't doubt that Rhosyn could handle the man. After several gulps, Krentz studied Brayden. "In six months or so after the Fleet has forgotten your little indiscretion, I'll inquire about reinstating your license. By then I'll have picked up a few more credits from playing Robard's Bluff with you." Krentz gave the woman a sloppy kiss and her shoulders tensed as she kissed him back.

Pulling away from Krentz, she glanced at Brayden. "I ordered another reading from Krakatan. I've been monitoring them every six hours. It doesn't look good. The planet won't last six months." She dropped her gaze as if knowing Krentz would disapprove of this news but knowing Brayden would need to hear this. "I estimate those colonists have about four weeks."

"Shit," Brayden said under his breath.

"What was your bet?" Krentz asked, getting back to the game, apparently unconcerned for the lives of the colonists. Rhosyn glanced at Krentz's cards then flashed Brayden a look, her green eyes seeming to hold a bit of sympathy. Brayden thought he almost detected the slightest shake of her head as if telling him not to bet.

The commander didn't have any tells, any habits that would give away what he had in his hand. If the commander's woman had a tell, Brayden might have a chance to win. It would be a daring and stupid move on her part if the woman was trying to help him cheat. Unless she was trying to help Krentz. She was too new for Brayden to know where her loyalties lay, although Brayden suspected that she didn't care much for Krentz. Recruits like her used their beauty to get ahead anyway they could on the Outer Rim. Staying in good favor with the commander of a large vessel like the *Valafar*, could secure her position and rank for a long time. What a way to promote your career. Even if he couldn't blame her for her career path, Brayden wasn't attracted to Rhosyn. Her manipulative charms didn't appeal to him.

Brayden thought about his own career, and he wasn't in any better shape, prostituting himself up the food chain in the Fleet. It was common among officers and got worse farther out. Transporting colonists, supplies, equipment and livestock sounded important, an honorable job in the Fleet, but he knew of the many dishonorable things he'd had to do to keep that position. Doing side jobs that would make your commander richer would put you on good standing with him, but also risked the wrath of the Fleet administrators if caught. Well, this time Brayden got caught. Who gets blamed for the illegal activity? Certainly not the commander. Damn Krentz.

"Raising a credit, I said."

"Hold on," the commander said as he laid his cards face down on the table to use both hands to fondle the woman.

The bastard was so confident he was winning the final hand. "Play your hand, man, I want to review the latest statistics on Krakatan."

"Forget about them. They're history. They were warned not to settle there. They didn't listen. They never do." Krentz laughed with no compassion.

"We're still responsible."

"No, you are." Krentz pointed at Brayden then picked up his cards frowning. "You follow orders, I make the bonus—"

"And people die," Brayden interrupted.

"They're not dead yet," the woman spoke up. "There are several fissures miles wide opening up, but the most violent volcanic activity hasn't reached the colony yet."

So the new hot crew member was an environmental scientist. "One month is accurate?" Brayden asked.

Her face looked grim. "At the most. Eruptions are occurring at various places around the planet. It could be less. I'm sorry."

Brayden nodded. Thirty colonists would die because of him. Because of his greedy Fleet commander and because naïve colonists were too eager to settle on a planet not yet cleared as safe.

"Brayden, consider your suspension a vacation," Krentz said in a conciliatory tone. "When the Fleet found out about our 'deals', someone had to be responsible. You'll get your license back in six months or a year. And in two years, your rank and pay will be back to where it was."

Brayden stared at him, and wiped at the sweat on his brow. "What do you have?" Cocking his head toward Krentz's cards. Krentz slowly turned the cards with a wicked grin. Brayden tossed his cards swearing under his breath. Of course the bastard beat his hand and won the pot. He lost his last Fleet Credit, and he'd have to borrow to make it through the next pay cycle. Krentz cackled and scooped up the pot of credit chips. He turned to the woman, grabbed her shirt and pulled her to him for another deep, juicy kiss, then slipped his hand under her skirt. The recruit rocked her hips and moaned.

Brayden cursed under his breath, wishing he could punch something like his commander's face.

"Hey, darling, meet me in my cabin," the commander said. "Get naked and send me a comm-pic of your pussy when you're ready for me." She stood, glancing at Brayden, giving him a wistful look.

"Sure. I'll be waiting." She left the common room. As Krentz counted his credits, Brayden stood to leave but his commander raised a hand to halt his retreat. Shoving the chair back under the table, Brayden finished his drink and let the sharp alcohol warm his belly. He hated to think what this woman was going to do only to advance her career. Perhaps it was also her way of survival.

If Brayden didn't love to fly so much, he would've burned his license years ago. But he couldn't imagine doing anything else, even in this isolated, lonely and dangerous place in the universe.

The Outer Rim was not the best place to find the company of a good woman. The last woman he had crossed paths with was Jaida Chel, a passenger from one of his transport trips. She was member of a colony relocated to an Outer Rim planet. Fortunately, that planet had been cleared and safe for colonization. Jaida was beautiful, hot, insatiable for sex and eager to please. They'd managed to do amazing things in his tiny bunk-sized cabin.

Planetside was not his idea of home. Being the son of a Fleet Commander, Brayden had traveled from planet to planet whenever his father was reassigned, spending more time on ships than land. A cramped bunk-sized cabin felt more like home. Then Brayden joined the Fleet and Jaida had arrived as one of his passengers.

His loins stirred as memories returned of his hot and wild passenger. Dammit, after all this time he could almost feel her going down on his cock, feel her tongue swirling around the head. Oh yes, she always came to his bunk naked and hungry for sex. Those times were a test in control, while he allowed himself to savor the pleasure before she took him over the brink. He'd enjoyed exploring her with his mouth, his fingers, his hands, from her upthrust breasts, down her belly to her slit. Remembering how she would jump when he'd pressed his tongue at the heart of her pleasure, made his cock hard.

Brayden could still taste her, feel her, could almost hear her moan. Damn. He had to stop torturing himself. Although Jaida was not a woman created for space flight, she did have the hard edges necessary to survive on an Outer Rim planet. The one thing he couldn't forgive her for was that she made him remember what he'd thought he'd forgotten long ago—having a woman in his life. He hadn't longed for someone for many years as a Fleet pilot. At least until he met Jaida. Now he couldn't stop thinking about her, couldn't stop trying to imagine the sights, scents, sounds, and especially the feel of her. A Fleet pilot had a lonely job, and it was the worst job to have for relationships.

Krentz stuffed his stack of credits into his shirt pocket so the bulge showed and leaned back in his chair, sipping his Cahoon Jack. "I have an assignment for you." He grinned.

Brayden groaned inside. The last assignment sent a dozen colonists to a volcanic planet and their death. "How can I do an assignment without my—"

"This one will get your license back."

Brayden knew this was a job he wasn't going to like. More than likely it would be worse than the Krakatan job. "I'm listening."

CHAPTER 2

Somerled

Jaida Chel slipped off her raw silk sarong and flung it over the hook on her kitchen wall. Now naked and cooler, she rushed back to the bubbling pot of blue-green slurry on her stove and waved her Applewood wand over the steaming brew, reciting a blessing as she stirred.

> *Oh, guardians of this distant land,*
> *protectors where the sargassia dwell,*
> *Infuse no ill nor bane for Somerled.*
> *I ask you to charge my magic spell.*

After lighting a candle and white sage incense on the counter next to the stove, she took a quick sip from her glass of lialade. The afternoon sun streamed in through her wide windows and open door raising the heat in her tiny adobe cottage. Outside the warm breeze rustled the leaves of her citrus trees and abundant garden of grapes, vegetables and herbs. Closing her eyes, she inhaled the sweet-scented breeze and enjoyed the brief swirling coolness on her bare skin.

Her nipples tightened and hardened to the gentle touch of air, like a lover's breath. It had been much too long since she'd made love—half a year on Somerled. What if she took a lover from town? Nothing permanent, just a casual affair. After three years on this planet, the colonists had forgiven her for her devastating mistake at the last settlement. Most agreed this was a more hospitable planet even if it wasn't their first choice.

It was all her fault they had to relocate here. The colonists had made the adjustment. If only she could forgive herself. She might find a willing partner now. Nothing serious. She doubted there would be a man from the colony willing to ostracize himself and be her life mate, but she might find a secret lover.

A few ideas came to mind on how she might accomplish such a plan. The only concerns were to keep the other colonists from finding out and making Kai understand her needs. Kai could be very difficult and jealous at times.

She glanced at her shelves containing jars and bottles of elixirs, teas and ointments that she sold or bartered with the colonists. Her Dragon Tear Elixir, the most prized product on Somerled for its medicinal purposes, was nearly out. To make more she had to travel to the coast for the sargassia harvest, the Elixir's key ingredient. Mmmm.

The twice a year harvest had its other benefits too— seeing Trent again. She smiled and her sex clenched. Noticing the layer of green slime on the surface of the bubbling mixture, she quickly skimmed it off with a flat spoon. The aquasam had to be poured into the containers before it jelled or she'd have one hell of a mess.

The warning bells clanged, signaling a guest approaching her house. The bells were her magical guard dog. The garden gate squeaked as heavy footsteps trod up her stone walkway.

She rolled her eyes to the ceiling and sighed. Mr. Moretti. Forgawdsake. She eyed her blue tunic hanging on the hook out of reach and then at the pot of aquasam that she dared not stop preparing. As the last of the thick skin was removed, she picked up the pot and began pouring it into the small jars. Caught naked in her kitchen again.

Was Mr. Moretti making a habit of arriving early on pick-up days, or was it her imagination? He distributed her wares in the village store since most colonists dared not visit her, and she avoided trips into the village unless absolutely necessary.

"Mr. Moretti, you're early. Could you wait outside? I'm almost finished." He didn't answer, but out of the corner of her eye, she saw a figure standing in her doorway. The dazzling sun peered into the house behind him, only allowing her to see his silhouette. She felt his gaze travel over every inch of her.

She dribbled a little of the blue-green syrup down one of the jars and groaned. "Grant me power," she mumbled, then called out to him. "You can leave my delivery at the door while I pack up your order." Still no answer.

Nudity wasn't uncommon among the settlers—Somerled was a tropical planet most of the year—but it wasn't exactly proper for a married man to be alone with a single woman, especially when she was naked. Then she heard two thunks outside her door—her bags of rice and flour. "Great. Have yourself a seat under the lia-lia trees, and I'll get you something to drink in just a minute." Already the solution was darkening and getting thick and hard to pour.

But the shadow remained, leaning casually in her doorway, arms crossed. Her cheeks heated and a shiver crept up her body. Mr. Moretti was a stout man and at least fifteen years her senior, not her type. And it was not like him to be so bold and impolite.

Finishing her chore, she turned to face him, a bit annoyed with his rudeness. But the man leaning casually in her doorway was not Mr. Moretti. He was tall, broad in the chest, with well-defined muscular arms and dark hair cut short.

With the sun so low in the sky Jaida could not see the man's face. Nor could she guess who he might be. She swallowed, took a step back as her mind raced trying to recall the other settlers in the village who could fit the dimensions of this man but couldn't.

A twinge of fear shot through her at the thought of space raids, but she hadn't heard the sirens. "Are…are you here to pick up Mr. Moretti's order?" she stammered. Who was this man? She glanced at her sarong, suddenly feeling exposed but hesitated to grab it because she wouldn't give him the satisfaction of showing her discomfort. "Did another freighter or shuttle arrive today?" she asked with her power voice, the confident tone used to evoke the goddess and nature spirits on this planet to do her spells.

The man chuckled. A familiar, sexy laugh. "Hello, Jaida."

Her stomach twirled with excitement, her nipples tightened and her body ached with need, all from the sound of his voice. Damn you, Captain Brayden Stokes. Her heart ached too, although she thought she'd put that part of their brief encounter all behind her.

She breathed in the white sage, burning in a censer, in an attempt to block the erotic memories of Brayden that flooded her mind—his mouth, his hands pleasuring her.

Closing her eyes, her thoughts drifted to many hot, passion-filled hours, making full use of every spare inch of his tiny, private bunk. She'd spent many lonely nights here on Somerled cursing him for leaving her.

An involuntary throb began between her thighs, remembering his hard cock plunging deep inside her. The sage did nothing to ease her desire. Already, she felt dampness between her thighs.

She was clean-shaven. If Brayden glanced down would he see the evidence that betrayed her desire? Crossing her arms over her waist in a casual pose, she then turned on an angle and crossed one ankle over the other in an attempt to hide her pussy. She glared at his silhouette.

"Hello, Brayden. What brings you planetside?" she asked coolly.

"Taking leave for a few months."

"Right," she drawled out. "As I recall, you hate setting your feet on solid ground. Always had to have several million gallons of flammable propellant shooting your ass all over the far ends of the galaxy."

He laughed. "I thought you liked my ass."

Biting her lower lip, trying not to smile, she thought about the time on board his ship when she snuck into his cabin and found him in the coffin-sized shower. She teased him about his cute ass. Before she knew it, he'd pulled her into the shower, clothes and all.

How they managed such frenetic lovemaking in that small space, she would never know. But it got her hot all over every time she thought of it. Of all the men she had slept with in her adult years, and the number of relationships or encounters, she couldn't remember one who'd groaned with as much pleasure. And it thrilled her to think she could bring a man to that state.

Goddess, she loved how it was with him in bed— stroking, touching, urgent needs, driven wild and intense, neither able to get enough of the other. She took a long, shuddering breath and walked to her sarong and slipped it over her head, securing the halter ties around her neck.

"Don't get dressed on my account."

Shaking her head, she glared at him as she walked past, picked up her bags of rice and flour and stepped back into her house. Three years hadn't changed him, including his wiseass attitude. She glanced at his full lips and instantly remembered bruising, incendiary kisses. Damn him for loving what he does. He would always be a space drifter. His heart moving much too fast for any woman to capture. She shook off the sensation of sinking in the algae swamp and gave him a cool stare.

"Got tired of the illegal trade business? Now, you're making deliveries for Moretti?"

"Legal goods, illegal trading," he corrected. "Colonists on the Outer Rim like you wouldn't survive otherwise."

"And you make quite a profit. So why are you here?"

He shrugged his shoulders. "I told Moretti I was looking for work and also looking for you. He handed me the bags then pointed me toward your house."

The short-sleeved, black shirt was completely unbuttoned showing off his muscular chest and flat abs. He also wore black pants and work boots—the Fleet pilot's uniform, plain, but very rugged and sexy. She closed her eyes and swore silently. She wasn't going to do this to herself again. He would be leaving in a day or so. Brayden was not the type to hang around.

"So when are you really leaving? Tomorrow?" Her tone had a bite to it, but she couldn't help it. He'd hurt her when he dropped her off and left, barely saying goodbye.

He raised his eyebrows, hesitating. "A few months."

She laughed. "Right. Outer Rim Fleet captains don't get a few months off—ever. I know you, Brayden. You're like a tiger that lives and hunts alone. And you have to keep moving. When it comes to space travel the more remote or insurmountable the journey, the better."

"There are more credits in the longer runs," he added.

"And no credits when you're planetside." She glared at him then lowered her voice. "What did you do? Did you kill someone?"

His expression darkened for a moment. He glanced away and murmured something she couldn't decipher.

She didn't miss the twitch of disgust at his jaw. When he turned back to face her, he took a breath, then smiled suggestively.

"C'mon, Jaida. It's been three years. Aren't you glad to see me?"

"Brayden, is that why you came up here? Just to get laid? I'm sure there are a few women in the village who'd be happy to accommodate you. I have work to do." She loaded the jars of aquasam in a burlap bag.

"What's that?"

"It's made from the algae in the swamps. The settlers use a ton of the stuff as an ointment for burns, cuts and sun protection, some say it's an aphrodisiac. Need some?" She smiled, teasing him.

"Working in the fields as farmers, I can see why," Brayden said, ignoring her dig.

"Not the life you're cut out for, hmm?" she snapped back.

"I love to fly but there's nothing wrong with being a settler. Now I'll get to try it for a while."

Jaida strode over to the empty cauldron used to brew the aquasam. The pot was cool enough now to clean, so she brought it to her sink. Brayden moved next to her while she worked.

"What else do you make?" He took the clean cauldron out her hand and dried it with a towel, and then set it on her small wooden table. Easing into one of her chairs, he pointed to one for her to do the same.

She dropped into a chair at the end of the table and met his gaze. "My Dragon Tear Elixir is my most popular product. It's vital for the colonists' survival because of its..." She hesitated and looked down at the table. "There's a mild poison in the air on Somerled, something the routine scans didn't pick up. Over several months, it caused purple spots on the skin. Dragon Tear Elixir cured the condition."

"You found an important contribution to secure your place here."

"Perhaps." They never would completely accept her though. They tolerated her because she had something they needed for survival, and that was all. If they didn't need her, they would find a way to banish her from Somerled.

He studied her for a long time, leaning back in his chair. She glanced around the room, suddenly at a loss for conversation and feeling the weight of his scrutiny. During the long passage between Mandara and Somerled, what did they talk about? They'd always managed to work around his busy schedule, monopolizing short blocks of time to be together. It wasn't all sex. They had talked, hadn't they?

Why were things so awkward now? Standing up, she strode to the burlap sack and carried it to the door. "You can bring this back to Mr. Moretti. He'll know what to do with it."

"Why did your colony leave Mandara? It was a fine planet, close to the shipping lanes, good climate, plenty of resources. And the native inhabitants agreed to small groups of settlers. Why did you pack up and move all the way the hell out here?" He came over to her, standing next to her.

She bit her lower lip and didn't answer.

Brayden continued. "I'd asked a few colonists during the passage to Somerled, and no one gave me a direct answer. They just said it didn't work out. Something about a skirmish with the natives."

Straightening her back, she stood close to him, clenching her teeth. "What game are you playing, Brayden?" She poked at his chest and quickly regretted it because she hit hard muscle and had a sudden urge to slide her hands over his body. "You don't want to settle here, you don't want...never mind." She took a step back, eyes blurring with tears.

Just when she'd almost stopped thinking about him for a day at a time, he'd come back into her life. "Isn't this where we left off three years ago?"

He nodded and reached out, grabbing her hands and pulling her into in his arms. No, she was not going to cry. He held her and stroked her back, nothing sexual, but her body wanted him and wanted him bad. Goddess, he felt good. She longed to melt into him, but resisted.

It would be too easy to get her emotions all tangled with Brayden again, only to have her heart crushed. She knew the moment she trusted him again, fell in love with him again, he'd leave. She'd wake up and he'd be gone. For a brief moment, the memory of watching his ship depart Somerled came back to her. Emptiness twisted inside her chest as if she experienced it all over again.

Brayden pressed his lips to her hair. His warm breath caressed her ear and neck. The despair of missing him all those years disappeared, as a desperate yearning took hold of her and sent a wave a heat through her. More than ever, she needed his mouth on hers, wanted to feel him naked and inside her again.

She sucked in a breath and gripped his arms. Holding him like this wasn't enough. She felt his arousal, although he didn't rub his thick cock against her. He could've and she knew she would respond. She always had in the past.

She sighed in resignation. "How long are you here for, honestly?" Once more, he'd managed to work his way into her life. Could she keep her emotions out of it this time?

Living on the Outer Rim was lonely, she had to capture the moments when they made themselves available. If she could keep her emotions out of the mix, this could be the hot casual fun she was looking for. She groaned to herself. There was never anything casual about Brayden. And this was the worse time with the sargassia needing harvesting. Brayden would not understand the harvesting ceremony. What about Kai? What about Trent?

He tangled his hand in her long brown hair and brushed his lips against her forehead. "Honestly, sweetheart. I'm here for a year."

She sucked in air. "My goddess, Brayden. What did you do?"

CHAPTER 3

Dragon Tears

Brayden ignored her question for the moment as he released her and strolled around the adobe-style home, admiring the simple furnishings and decorations, seeing her crafty touches. The colorful handwoven baskets and rugs he knew she did herself. The rough-pressed earthen walls and stone floors must keep the house cool most of the day and retained heat on cool nights.

He wiped sweat from his brow and willed his cock to settle down. In another moment, he would've had her pinned down on the bed. Show a little restraint. "I saw solar panels on the roof. Is that your main source of power?"

She made an impatient face and rolled her eyes. He wouldn't get away with avoiding her question for long. He hadn't really lied to her about being assigned there for a year. Krentz had given him six months to a year to complete his mission. "Solar isn't the only source, but our main one. We're down to the basics here."

"You do quite well." He saw her bedroom in a little alcove off the main room. That shared space included a modest kitchen, eating and lounging area, and that was it. Simple and efficient. Did she spend her nights alone in that bed? "Why is your place so far from the village?"

Her cottage was a twenty-minute walk from the main colony and up a steep hill. She glanced at him with a guarded look. A look he remembered well, that usually meant she was hiding something.

"You remember how I don't like closed-in places. I also like the view and the colonists aren't crazy about some of my methods for making my products."

"But you're a biologist."

"And Wiccan. I tend to mix a little science and magic. And a few other things."

He remembered her doing rituals in her cabin during the transport, but she kept to herself mostly, and he pretty much ignored them. Guess his mind was on her body, not on her religious beliefs. "And the colonists don't approve?"

"They tolerate it only because of the Dragon Tear Elixir."

"They're superstitious?"

"Yes, they believe I infused my product with witchcraft, something magical so that the product has a use other than what was intended. Like aphrodisiac properties in the Elixir."

"They shouldn't complain," Brayden said. "I heard soon after your arrival creatures destroyed crops and food was scarce."

Jaida shot him a look. "The dragons destroyed most of the first crops, because we plowed and irrigated their lands. We invaded their homes. We had plenty of packaged food to get us through."

"Sentient?"

Jaida nodded. "But it was too late. The killing had started and the dragons were fighting for their lives. I was at the coast collecting plants for my herbal medicines and lotions. I missed most of it."

Stepping closer, he grasped her hands. He wanted to pull her into his arms again, slip that thin wrap over her head, and make love to her. But it had been a few years. He breathed in her scent—citrus and sweet herbs. And all the hot, passionate nights on his ship flooded his memory. He willed his cock to ignore the fantasies. The material of her wrap clung to every curve, and her nipples poked so invitingly through the fabric. It was taking all his willpower not to put his mouth over the peaks and suck, then apply a little pressure with his tongue. "I'm glad you weren't in the area during the fight. Was anyone killed?"

"Two colonists. A doctor and a carpenter. A devastating loss for the settlement."

"You're doing okay now?"

She nodded and squeezed his hands, even leaned into him a bit. Being this close to her was killing him. In the three years since he'd brought her to Somerled, he hadn't met another woman who was such a wildcat, who was soaking wet with desire the moment she hopped into his bunk. Fuck, she filled those millions of lonely miles with a rush of new and exciting adventures.

Making love with Jaida was like hovering on the edge of a black hole, not knowing what mysteries or dangers were beyond, but desperately wanting to risk the chance to discover them. Maybe he had leapt into that black hole after all and lost his heart in oblivion. Not a chance.

He hadn't been able to forget her. Jaida was right. He did like to keep moving, but it was more than the sex. He admired her fearlessness and independence. Not many women journeyed this far alone. "This is a comfortable house," he said studying her eyes, and trying to determine if she welcomed his visit. Their parting hadn't been on the best of terms.

She looked around and smiled with pride. "It's small, but it's mine, and I have my place in society. They've accepted me, considering my past mistakes."

"Not as small as my bunk on the ship." He wagged his eyebrows at her and was grateful when she smiled back.

"Very true, but I remember we made good use of the space." Even the captain on a commercial Fleet vessel got few perks. His quarters weren't much larger than his crew's. It was about the size of a large closet. He did have a private bath. One of his favorite sexual positions with Jaida had required him to stand partway into the bathroom, close to the bed, while she lay on her back, legs spread. He'd pumped his cock into her and got a lot of leverage.

"That we did."

Hell, he wanted her now. His cock swelled and he ached to adjust himself, but knew it would look much too obvious. "Can I bother you for something to drink?"

"Oh, of course. I'm sorry. Lialade?"

"And that is?" He followed her to her small refrigerator.

"Those trees I have outside are lia-lia trees that bear a citrus fruit similar to lemon and lime." He nodded and watched as she filled a glass with ice and the pale green juice, and his eyes roamed over her body. Her round, full breasts swayed beneath the thin material. Her nipples puckered, showing every detail down to the areolas. He ached to suck them and make them even tighter. The thought made his cock grow harder still.

The hem of her sarong barely skimmed the bottom of her ass and the material clung between her legs. Was her pussy wet? He wanted to touch her, and taste her. Fuck, he was torturing himself. "I need a job, Jaida. I'm stuck here until I can get my pilot's license back. Mr. Moretti hired me to work the bogs and the fields, run errands. He said you needed help gathering plants for your medicines and herbal preparations. How much do you pay?" He grinned at her.

She pursed her lips, considering his offer. "I have a tough time getting any of the villagers to come with me to the coast. It's a two-day journey, and I need to lug back the dried sargassia kelp I use for the Dragon Tear Elixir."

"I heard Moretti say everyone is almost out. I thought this planet was screened for atmospheric toxicity. Occasionally few planets do get approval when they shouldn't, credits change hands—but I thought Somerled was cleared," Brayden said, knowing all too well the corruption he had to deal with in the Fleet.

Jaida's mouth twitched as she poured herself a drink. She swirled the green juice around in the glass. "The levels of heavy metals in the air, soil and water are acceptable, but measurable enough to cause harm over time. I've done studies and Dragon Tear Elixir helps to detoxify the body of these elements." She narrowed her eyes at him as if expecting him to argue.

"I see."

"More lialade?" She held up her glass and smiled.

He shook his head. "Why don't the villagers want to come to the coast to help you?"

"It's a long and rugged journey like I said. They don't like the challenge of adventure or to leave their crops." She turned back with a confident, sultry smile in place. "It's just your kind of job. Are you up for it? I'll pay you the same as I pay the villagers—in food and herbal products."

"Sounds like more fun than working in a rice bog or the fields."

She laughed and put down her drink. "I wouldn't say more fun, but it is more exciting."

"Count me in." He downed his drink. "When do we leave?"

"Tomorrow. But first…" She sidled her body against him until his cock pressed painfully hard against her mound. "We don't let things go to waste around here, Brayden. Three years is a long time. Aren't we going to make good use of that?"

Brayden fisted his hand in her hair and crushed her mouth with a scorching kiss. Everything soft and hard responded to his touch. A primal lust overwhelmed him. He didn't know where to begin pleasuring her, where to begin exploring. He'd been wanting to do that from the moment he saw her.

A satisfying moan escaped her lips as their mouths parted briefly. Her hands ravished him, yanked off his shirt, pulled at his belt, then dug inside his pants where she gripped his shaft so hard, he jerked from the slight pain.

"You want me?" she whispered against his mouth, taking her hand out of his pants.

He answered with a deep groan. Oh, hell. Every stroke practically sent him over the edge. "Jaida, sweetheart," he murmured as he buried his mouth in her neck, tasting the salt on her skin and smelling incense and citrus in her hair. He reached under her sarong and slid his fingers up along her thigh to finger her shaved pussy. Her body trembled when he reached her swollen bud, rolled his finger around it and slipped his fingers between her folds. "Yes, I knew you'd be wet. You were always wet when you came to me," he said huskily.

"Brayden, mmmm yes, that's so good." She rocked her hips against his hand. "Take these off," she demanded as she tugged on his pants.

Before he complied, he thrust a finger deep inside her and relished in the sound of her breath catching. She gripped his shoulders and drowsily gazed in his eyes. Her exotic hazel eyes shone with that glassy, wildcat look he knew so well. She fumbled with his pants.

"I want your cock inside me, and I want to be lying down. Take your pants off now," she demanded again, this time impatiently.

He laughed. "Okay, I get the message." He realized he still had on his work boots. With shaky hands, he unlaced and kicked them off, then slid out of his pants. Jaida had already pulled her sarong off in one motion and tossed the silky material on the floor. She drew him toward the bed. Slow and romantic never did describe their lovemaking in the past. More like impulsive, dangerous, even savage and out of control. He expected their lovemaking planetside wouldn't be any different. When they got to her bed, she pushed him down and pounced on top of him, pinning his arms on either side of his head.

The abruptness surprised him, but he didn't argue. He chuckled softly as she came down and found his mouth for a bruising kiss, but she didn't release his arms. He loved her aggressive, take-charge attitude. All that bouncing around would not have worked in his tiny bunk cube on the ship. If she had tried that maneuver on the ship, she would've knocked herself out. Go for it, sweetheart. Instead of straddling him and impaling his engorged cock deep inside her, she slithered down his body, touching, stroking and kissing her way down to his crotch.

His body hungered to feel her secret depths, but equally ached for her mouth, remembering how well she could pleasure him. She gripped his shaft in her hand then took him in her mouth, flicking the head and rim with her tongue, then slid down, taking most of the length deep into her throat.

"Oh God, Jaida. So good." It was surreal. Any minute he would awaken on his ship, having another wet dream about her. Slipping his hands into her hair, he felt the silkiness and stroked her shoulders. Damn, slow down. He had to take deep breaths to keep from coming. He could smell her tangy, sweet arousal, mixed with the citrus scent floating in on the breeze that whisked away the beads of perspiration on his skin. Nope, he wasn't dreaming, thank God. "Slow it down, sweetheart, or I'm done," he whispered.

Cupping his balls, she slipped one into her mouth. A ripple of intense sensations moved up from his groin. He tightened his muscles to hold off the orgasm. He slid his hands under her shoulders and drew her up. "Come to me so I can taste you."

She knelt on either side of his shoulders, her legs spread wide for him. He grabbed her ass, pulled her close and sucked on her tender folds. Jaida gripped the wooden headboard for support and quivered beneath his mouth. She moaned as he increased the pressure. His tongue teased her clit while his finger gained entrance and found his mark and pressed. "Yes, yes, like that." She groaned and rocked her hips in tiny movements, matching his rhythm.

He eagerly strummed her bud, keeping the pressure gentle and teasing. Then her body shook convulsively as she climaxed. He wrapped his arm around her hips and continued the pressure on her pussy until her cries quieted. "Hmm. So nice." Then he flipped her on her back and nudged the head of his cock at her wet cleft.

Raising her hips, she opened for him, but he only let the tip enter a little. She moaned her complaint, her body twitching beneath him, and attempted to raise her hips higher. "Stop teasing me and come inside."

"Feisty little thing, aren't you?"

"You have no idea, if you don't get down to business," she said between panting breaths. Hovering above her, hands on either side of her, he slid his cock along her slit and enjoyed feeling her quivering in agony.

"You want me?"

"Forgawdsake, yes. Take me."

He laughed under his breath. "Enough torture for now." He plunged deep into her. She arched her back and cried out. Her legs wrapped around his hips, limiting his movements, but his thrusts were deep and hard and fast. He sealed his mouth over hers for a brief kiss, then broke away as they both gasped for breath. He slowed his breathing, holding off just a little longer. He could tell by her breathing and the clenching on his cock that she must be close.

"Brayden, yes, oh yes." Then her back arched, she groaned and her body shook beneath him. Her hands roamed along his chest, and he again focused on his own body, the pressure building and suddenly thrust him into a shattering climax. "Oh God, Jaida."

Sensations racked his body. Every muscle pulsing and thrumming with searing pleasure. When their heart rate and breathing wound down to more normal pacing, he collapsed beside her and she curled against his chest.

Sometime later, Jaida asked as she drew circles on his chest. "As good as you remember?"

He shrugged. "It'll do, I suppose. I miss my bunk on the ship." He mashed his lips together holding back a smile.

She stopped drawing her circles and rose on her elbow to look at him, her hazel eyes blazing. When she saw the smile that he couldn't contain, she punched his arm. "Creep."

"Ouch."

"You deserved it. I like the extra space by the way. I don't have to worry about banging my head or elbows."

"Have to agree. Nice bed." He pulled her down, stroking her hair. "I've missed you." She was the one woman who could tempt him into moving planetside—almost.

He pulled her close and drew in a deep breath. The smell of burning wood drifted into the house. Twisting out of his arms, Jaida flew out of bed and ran naked outside.

"Brayden, help me! Get a bucket of water! Kai, no!"

Brayden jumped out of bed and raced after Jaida. Flames streaked up the branches of one of her lia-lia trees, charring the bark, leaves and precious fruit.

The tree stood in the middle of her garden surrounded by neat rows of vegetables and herbs, but nothing else had caught fire yet.

He shook his head at the odd sight. "Ow." Still naked and barefoot, he'd stepped on a sharp stone as he padded across her yard searching for something that would hold water.

"There, Brayden, by the pond, fill the bucket. Hurry." She pointed at the far end of her house where a shallow pool was overgrown with weeds and algae. "Damn it, Kai. I told you we're leaving tomorrow."

Grabbing another bucket from a tool shed, she scooped water from the pond and tossed the contents onto the flames. Brayden added one more bucketful right behind hers, dousing the last of the flames. Smoke coiled into the air as she examined the damage.

Standing next to the scorched tree was a dragon. Brayden took a step back and let out a low whistle. The creature stood a couple of heads taller than he when it stood straight up and had bronze, reptilian skin. Leathery wings flapped as its mouth opened, showing sharp teeth. Glowing green eyes watched Jaida and Brayden as they finished extinguishing the burning branches.

The creature took a step forward, tilted its head and glared at Brayden. Brayden didn't dare take his eyes off it. Out of its snout came puffs of gray-black smoke. It prowled along the edge of the garden, spewing small streams of flames from its mouth.

Brayden thought it would take off flying or start another fire. Fortunately, the house was made from mostly packed earth and stone, or that too would've gone up in flames.

So, Fleet Commander Krentz was right. The colonists hadn't destroyed all the dragons on Somerled.

CHAPTER 4

Needful Things

Jaida plucked charred leaves and scorched fruit from the damaged tree and placed them in a container for her compost pile. "Kai, this will take at least two seasons to grow back," she yelled at the dragon. The creature stood quietly inside the garden, head lowered and breathing deeply. She had never seen him this upset before. "No wonder the villagers don't want you near them."

Brayden watched her work, cleaning up the charred remains of her fruit tree. He frowned as if in deep thought. He did look rather magnificent standing naked in her garden, despite the loss of one of her trees. Kai could've destroyed her entire garden in a few seconds, but he knew she depended on the crops to survive.

And he depended on her for his survival.

"I heard the colonists had killed off all the dragons on Somerled." He stepped around Kai in a wide circle, studying him like a scientist.

The dragon's long neck twisted around, following Brayden. Kai's eyes narrowed. She held her breath, waiting to see if the two males would challenge each other. "When we first arrived, the settlers almost destroyed them all. Kai is the last of his kind."

"Why were they killed?"

"Because the dragons burned the fields and injured the villagers. I convinced the villagers to stop."

Brayden frowned. "Destroying crops could mean a colony starves, so I can understand their logic."

"Not a reason to annihilate a whole species."

Kai whimpered and wheezed, taking in a deep breath. Jaida held up her hand in warning. "Don't you dare."

Kai released his breath slowly and sat on the ground with a grunt, his wings folded down behind him. The sight of two naked people standing in a garden with a dragon would've looked strange if a villager had arrived at that moment.

"And how did you convince the locals not to kill Kai?" Brayden stroked Jaida's hair, his eyes shone with concern.

She turned away from Brayden and faced Kai. The sooner she brought Kai to the coast the better. "I have a degree in herbal medicine and botany, but I also practice folk or nature magick. I discovered that dragon's fire enhanced the properties of the sargassia kelp and when taken internally on a regular basis, will detoxify the body of the harmful elements in the atmosphere.

"Dragon Tear Elixir is the most important potion I make, but I'm also learning to manifest other forces as they are specific to this planet. This isn't Earth, so the workings are different."

Kai slunk along the ground, glancing at Jaida now and then as if he knew he'd done something wrong. His bronze-colored scales shimmered in the golden afternoon light. His wings remained folded down at his sides and his tail dragged on the ground.

Brayden tilted his head toward the dragon. "You're his guardian."

"Yes, but he keeps us alive. It'll take us a few days to collect and dry the sargassia kelp at the coast. I appreciate you coming with me to help."

Brayden glanced sideways at Kai. "No problem. I need the work and it beats farming."

She picked a few ripe fruit that weren't harmed and placed them in a basket to pack for their trip the next day. "You'll have to make your delivery to Mr. Moretti first."

"Come with me and give me the official tour of the village."

"Fine." Her response was more abrupt than she'd intended, but going into town made her uncomfortable.

"Jaida, why did you come to this planet? Why did you come to the Outer Rim? There are much nicer planets closer to Earth, a bit more civilized."

Not turning to face him, she continued to pile finger-bananas, handfuls of red berries and strolled toward her vegetable garden to dig up a few carrots.

"My brother and I were part of this colony on Mandara. After he was killed, I was alone and couldn't imagine taking a chance with a colony of people I didn't know at all. When they decided to relocate, they still needed a botanist badly enough they were willing to pay my way. And they didn't mind me practicing magick or my esoteric methods for making medicines."

"What about your parents? I remember you telling me about them on the ship. Don't you miss them?"

Jaida put the basket down and glared at Brayden. "My parents don't want to have anything to do with me."

"What happened to your brother? You didn't tell me this on the ship." He took several steps toward her, but she put up her hand.

"Another time, Brayden. Can you get my sarong, please?"

His shoulders slumped and he nodded slowly, then turned and went inside her house. Walking over to the garden bench in the shade, Jaida plopped down and stared in disgust at the still smoldering fruit tree. With his head bowed low, Kai inched his way over and rested his chin on her lap, his emerald green eyes looked up at her with remorse. She stroked his rough, slick skin. "Is this because we didn't leave today? Or is it because of Brayden?" she asked the dragon. Kai blinked. He huffed a puff of smoke out of his nostrils in answer. "Don't do it again," Jaida demanded. "This harms the whole settlement, not just me."

Kai moaned.

* * *

They walked down the narrow path toward town. Jaida moved ahead of Brayden and picked up her pace. He couldn't figure out why she was in such a rush. "Are we running a race?" Brayden asked.

"We need to get packed and leave for the coast as soon as possible," she said without pausing. In the distance, farm land stretched out to the north and beyond that, a jagged mountain range reached into clouds. Marsh land covered most of the south side where the villagers grew rice. The varied landscape and warm temperatures provided an idea living environment for the colony. Not all frontier planets were as hospitable.

When they stepped onto the main street of the town, four colonists approached them from the other direction. When they saw her, they crossed the street and continued walking on the opposite side.

"What's that all about?" Brayden asked.

"Let's just make this delivery." They walked past many simple buildings—the sturdy, yet prefabricated homes for new settlements that looked like trailers with curved roofs. Mr. Moretti's general store stood at the end of one street. They entered. The smell of baked bread and simmering stew permeated the store. Several shelves lined the walls with textiles like clothes, linens and material. Other shelves contained fresh food items, canned goods and Jaida's products. Mr. Moretti sat on a tall stool behind a narrow counter arranging a tray of flatbread and muffins. "Mr. Moretti, I have your delivery," Jaida said.

Brayden propped the burlap bag of vials, jars and bottles onto the counter.

"Why did you come to town? I hired the captain so you wouldn't have to. Did he get lost?" Mr. Moretti walked out from behind the counter.

"I asked Jaida to give me a tour. I'll be going with her to the coast so she can collect herbs to make her products."

Mr. Moretti frowned, then nodded. "The sargassia. Yes, she could use the help, and we need the elixir. Be careful traveling through the marshland. It's dangerous. And don't trust her dragon. Maybe you'll tell us about your journey when you return."

The next day they started out for the coast before dawn. The air was cool and humid. Within a few hours the heat would slow their travel. By mid-morning, Brayden slipped the backpack off his shoulders and dropped it onto the ground while he retrieved his water and surveyed the area.

They'd been walking several hours and he couldn't find a clearing that would accommodate a shuttle. The thick tropical foliage, tall evergreen trees and marshy, swampy ground would make a landing impossible. Accomplishing his mission was going to be difficult.

"Why are you stopping?" Jaida asked.

"Getting a drink." He retrieved his water container from his pack and took a long drink. "Go on, I'll catch up." He would have to wait until they reached an open area before he called the ship. After Jaida turned around and disappeared with Kai, Brayden checked his Comm-device for an update on Krakatan and its inhabitants. His commander had left three messages.

Krakatan had minor eruptions, but the colony was out of harm's way for the moment. Reports said they had several days at the most before the volcanic activity destroyed the majority of the land masses. He considered telling Jaida his situation, but couldn't risk her not agreeing.

"Let's scoot, Brayden. Sunlight's burning," she yelled back to him. "We need to set up camp soon."

Brayden ran to them and noticed the dragon, chomping on a fan-shaped palm as the creature plowed through the tropical brush, breaking vines and branches in his path. "He keeps quite a pace," Brayden said. "Does he know the way?"

"He does, but I marked the trail with cairns, those stacks of stones, on the last couple of trips as trail markers." She pointed to small piles of stones about a foot high. "So you could find your way back? You don't need the dragon to lead you?" He walked past her, keeping the dragon in sight.

"Yes, I could find my way. And Kai is his name," she corrected him annoyed.

"Good. You wouldn't want to get lost out here."

"What's up, Brayden?" She grabbed his arm, pulling him to a stop.

"What's Kai to you? Is he like a pet?" He gave her an awkward smile but stopped when he saw anger flash across her expression.

"Kai is not my pet." And she left it at that. No help. Brayden had hurt her before, but he'd never betrayed her.

"Just asking. It's just that we're out in the middle of nowhere. If he were to run off… Neither of us has a GPS."

She finally smiled and shook her head. "Don't worry about Kai. You navigate by the skies at night, I'll navigate by the ground and landmarks. Kai won't get lost, he'll lead most of the way. You won't get lost as long as you don't wander off." She waved her wand over one of the cairns—the third time he saw her do that.

"Guess not. And what's the significance of the wand action over the pile of stones?"

"Cairns are places of power. They concentrate the energies of the stones and connect to the earth or planet. By waving my wand, I'm connecting my spirit and physical body with the planet's energies."

"Oh."

She laughed. "According to Brayden Stokes, if it's not measured by physics or calculus it doesn't exist."

He groaned. "That's not true. I'm open-minded about a lot of things."

"You are? I certainly hope so." She smiled wickedly.

What was he missing? He didn't think he would be around long enough to find out. Jaida was smart and a skilled witch. Brayden wondered how the dragon bonded to her and not with the others in the colony.

"Kai goes with you on every trip?"

"The coast was his home. We return once or twice a year to collect the sargassia. He's the one... I discovered the sargassia when Kai took me there."

"He helps you make it? But you don't really need him, do you?" Brayden asked as he sipped water.

She shot him a look. "Of course, I need him. His breath has a chemical reaction with the components in the kelp. It wouldn't be viable without him."

Kai took off flying, heavy wings flapping, and circled around then landed about a hundred yards in front and waited until they caught up. He grumbled as if calling to them to hurry.

"Why don't you just fly on him to the coast and collect what you need instead of walking?"

She turned and gave him an exasperated look. "Kai can't carry me and all the supplies for that distance. And there's not much fresh water by the coast. That's why we must lug it in. I dry the sargassia kelp at the shore, so there's less bulk to carry back."

"No one lives there?" She crossed her arms and glared at him. Brayden glanced at her from the side as they continued to walk, expecting for her to tell him more about this journey, but she didn't.

The sound of trickling water caught his attention, the first sign of a creek or river. Palm trees and lush foliage surrounded a tropical pond, fed by a crystal, clear stream and a small waterfall. Like a drink of cool water to a man crossing the desert, he couldn't remember the last time he took a swim. Seven, eight years old with his parents?

His mother rarely contacted him after he joined the Fleet. She and his dad split about the same time. The spouse of Fleet service personnel lived a secure but lonely life. Spouses couldn't travel on board the ships. Accommodations on a vessel were limited to crew and colonists. Fleet personnel saw their spouses during month-long leaves once a year.

His dad's transport vessel crashed into a docking bay and he was killed when the man was only forty-five.

"Look at that," Brayden said.

Jaida let out an exasperated huff and dropped her backpack on the ground, then retrieved a bag of dried fruit. "Fine, go take a look."

He ran over the edge of the pond and peered into deep water. "It's crystal. Looks about twenty feet deep." Kai stood on the edge next to Brayden.

"It's twice that," Jaida said. "It's drinkable too. We should fill our bottles while we're here." She carried her container toward Brayden and Kai.

Brayden swirled his hand in the water. "Feels cool. Nice." He kicked off his boots and stripped off his shirt. "Is it safe?" Brayden asked Kai.

"What are you doing?" Jaida asked, alarm in her voice. Kai nodded, swinging out a wing as if to say, "Go on in." Brayden swung his arms and bent his knees as he leapt out into a dive.

"No!" Jaida cried.

The cool, refreshing water rushed over his skin. He surfaced and squinted at the brilliant sunlight piercing through the waving palm fronds and shouted at Jaida. "This is great. Come on in."

Jaida screamed and pointing behind him. "Swim to shore, Brayden, hurry!"

"Why? What's wrong?" Kai stood beside Jaida, his head hanging low. "Damn it, Brayden. The pond is filled with crocodile-like creatures—man-eaters. There's one moving toward you." She screamed again.

"Kai, help him." She shoved at the dragon, but he didn't move, only cocked his head, glaring at Brayden with one eye. Brayden kicked and glanced over his shoulder as he began swimming toward shore. A creature about six feet long emerged from the shadows of overhanging vegetation and slithered in an S pattern across the surface of the water directly at Brayden.

"Oh, shit."

"Kai, please." Jaida placed a hand on her companion's shoulder, but the dragon huffed and flopped down on the ground, looked the other way, refusing to move. "Damn you, Kai. Oh, goddess, he's not going to make it."

The water creature gained on Brayden. She threw rocks out toward the enemy, barely missing Brayden. He appreciated her efforts, but it didn't seem to help. The crocodile thing thrashed a bit, but it didn't slow him down. "Hurry, it's right behind you." Brayden focused on Jaida and not on the predator pursuing him. His lungs ached, his muscles cramped, but he increased the speed of his strokes.

If he was going to die, he wanted her to be the last thing he saw. Right now, he saw the terror in her eyes and wished he could take the fear away. Wished he could hold her again. A whoosh and a dark shadow passed over his head. As he glanced up, massive leathery wings soared over his head and arc down toward the water beast.

Kai expelled a stream of smoke and flames across its path. The creature thrashed and stopped its pursuit, then spun around and retreated into the cover of the trees. Brayden didn't glance back again or slow his pace.

CHAPTER 5

Water Spell

"Why did you lose your license? And don't ignore me this time, or I'll have Kai throw you back into that pond."

Brayden's gut twisted in a painful knot, watching Jaida pull her hair back in a ponytail, her breasts jutting out against the tight cloth of her sarong. His cock stirred with recent memories, and he ached to take her again. "I made an illegal delivery. You know how it is with the Fleet. Someone wants some luxury item like food, water, medicine, agricultural items or women."

Jaida narrowed her eyes as she walked past, waving her wand in the air over her head. "And you do this for credits?" she asked with disgust.

"No, I do it to keep my job. My superiors give an order, even though it's not a legal flight or the supplies haven't been paid for. If I don't make these deliveries or pickups, they cut back my flights and my pay. And if I get caught, it's my fault and I take the blame."

"All this is so they can make an extra buck?"

"Some of the jobs and deliveries are frivolous bootleg items, exotic wares and such. The higher up you go in the Fleet, the more corrupt it gets. If you don't go along, you don't keep flying."

Jaida shook her head. "Nice business you're in."

"But I love to fly, and the job market is pretty scarce out here." Weaving in and out a dense group of evergreen trees, Jaida slowed her pace. Nearly out of sight, Kai dashed around the next curve in the trail.

"The Fleet corruption is bad enough, but how do you deal with all the diverse cultures on the various planets? Isn't it dangerous?"

She glanced behind her looking for his response. He shrugged. "Sometimes. But we're given Current Laws and Customs Data Sheets for each planet."

"Because you could make a mistake. Break a law and not know that you've broken one. It could be something simple, meaningless." Her voice rose and cracked. The pained look on her face tore at his heart.

"What is it, Jaida?" He grabbed her hand and pulled her to stop. She tried blinking back the tears.

"Okay, I'll tell you. When I first settled on the planet Mandara, I discovered rare medicinal herbs for my elixirs, so I collected a basket full. I found them at the edge of this forest. I didn't know I was trespassing on the native peoples' land. They captured me."

Brayden gasped. "Did they harm you?"

She shook her head. "My brother negotiated for my release. But I didn't realize, negotiating meant his life for mine. He was executed. For picking fucking flowers!"

Brayden took her into his arms and stroked her hair while the tears fell. "Your brother was a brave man. And your parents blame you?"

She nodded into his chest. He made a sound of disgust and bit back the words he wanted to say against her parents. Didn't they know she probably lived with the nightmare of her brother's execution every day?

Pulling away from him, she wiped at her eyes and started walking. "The Outer Rim isn't far enough away from Mandara."

"I understand." They walked for another couple hours. The jungle and marshy ground became dryer and less dense with vegetation. After passing several trail markers, something pungent assailed his nose. "What's that smell?" he asked. "Kai setting something on fire again?"

"Mineral springs. We'll stop here for the night." Jaida dropped her backpack on the ground and approached a small pool of steaming blue-green water. The bottom of the pond appeared white, probably from salt mineral deposits.

"Can we jump in?" Brayden asked, anxious to get the dust and sweat off him.

"Yes, but in a minute. I need to do a ritual." She still seemed pissed. Taking her wand out of her backpack, she drew symbols in the white sand next to the steaming mineral pool.

"What's that?"

"Shhh." She sat cross-legged beside the pool and took several breaths, then leaned forward and gazed into the water. Brayden started walking toward her, but Kai dropped down in front of him, blocking his path. His wings spread wide as if in a challenge and warning not to go farther.

"Okay, Kai, I get the message." The dragon seemed to understand because he lowered his wings, but didn't take his piercing green gaze off him. Brayden saw a flash of movement and heard Jaida mumble something.

She leapt to her feet, still staring into the pool. Then she picked up a pebble and tossed it into the water and pointed with her finger. Her lips counted silently. She frowned and made a fist, then picked up another pebble and tossed it in, then again began counting. And two more pebbles. She swore and spun around and headed into the dense growth of palms and pine trees.

"Jaida, what's wrong?" Brayden charged after her and caught up in a few strides.

She continued the march, ignoring him. "You're not staying the full year. You lied to me."

"How do you know that?"

"Water gazing and water spell. I saw you leaving and I counted the rings when I tossed in the pebbles. I asked if you were staying the full year and counted an even number of rings—a no."

He shook his head, confused.

"A form of divination. Forget it," she snapped. "I should've known things wouldn't change.

She'd tossed in four pebbles. What else did she ask? And how accurate was her magic?

"Maybe the Fleet will reissue my license sooner. If they need me, it's possible. I could leave sooner." He really wasn't lying to her, just not being completely honest. Hell, he was lying. Again, what choice did he have? "C'mon, Jaida. Don't worry about this." He picked up his pack. "We can get in a few more miles before it gets dark," he said cheerfully.

She shook her head as she started to unpack a small tent. "No. We'll camp here for the night." Was she deliberately delaying their trip? How much time did the colonists on Krakatan have before their planet became one giant mass of erupting volcanoes?

A planet named after Krakatoa should've been an omen. But the colonists paid the Fleet an enormous fee to take them to a planet not yet approved by scientists to be safe for colonization. Safe, hospitable planets were rare and usually claimed quickly. This group of colonists had chosen to take a chance before it was cleared and claimed it as their own. And Brayden took them there.

Now he needed to rescue them before it was too late. "The sun won't set for an hour or two, why don't we walk a bit longer."

"Last place for fresh water and night comes quickly once the sun sets. Come and soak in the mineral bath. Your muscles won't ache as much tomorrow." With a flip of her hand, the tent popped into shape. It was just large enough for two. She then slipped out of her sarong, kicked off her sandals and eased into the water.

He groaned as he watched the water inch up her legs, touch her sex, then flow up her belly. She stood waist-deep in the steaming spring, and splashed water on her breasts. Ugh. He was done for. He yanked his shirt over his head, kicked off his boots and dropped his pants. His engorged cock sprang free.

"Are there benefits to bathing in mineral water?" He smiled slyly.

She nodded, her expression strained with worry.

"I'll join you in just a minute." He walked behind a thick growth of vegetation as if he needed to relieve himself. With his Comm-device in hand, he called up the current conditions on Krakatan. Several mantle plumes and divergent tectonic plates detected. Colonists out of range of lava flow for next ninety-six hours.

Brayden rubbed his forehead. He knew his commander wouldn't offer the dangerous rescue mission to another captain under any circumstances, and even if one volunteered, he doubted there was another Fleet captain close enough to make the journey in time.

Only Brayden could rescue them, only he would be responsible. And what he had to do would destroy his friendship with Jaida forever. The idea of betraying her clawed at his chest. What a way to make a living.

Brayden sent a message to the commander saying his mission would be complete by tomorrow. Send the shuttle. He returned to the pool. Jaida floated on her back in the water, water swirling seductively around her breasts and pussy. She had her eyes closed, looking more relaxed. He slid into the heated water beside her. Opening her eyes, she sighed and frowned at Brayden. With the tip of his finger he stroked her shoulder and down her back, easing the tension.

She shivered and a smile twitched at her mouth. Kai slumped in the grass under a pine tree and grunted, glaring green eyes at Brayden, looking annoyed again. Brayden grasped her arm and pulled her across his lap. "Does he have to watch?"

"Kai?" She waved her hand and Kai leapt to his feet and loped into the woods. The hot water bubbled up between the smooth rocks and caressed Brayden's skin. The sulfur smell wasn't pleasant, but the water felt good. Jaida's breasts bobbed on the surface of the water. The sight instantly made him hard and aching.

"A short break, then we can eat." She wiggled her bottom against his cock, teasing, tempting him. Bastard. She shouldn't give in to him so easily, but he would be leaving soon so why not take pleasure when the opportunity arose? He'd always been honest with her, never made promises that he might break. She hadn't been completely honest with him about Kai.

When they got to the sea, she would explain everything—well, maybe not everything. "Careful, this won't be that short a break if you keep doing that," he said as he took her mouth and plunged his tongue deep. She moaned and climbed up, facing him and mounted him in one swift movement. "Oh, God, Jaida. Is there no satisfying you?" He gripped her hips and rose to reach even deeper.

"You aren't complaining, are you?"

"Never, sweetheart." She rocked on him, her fingers digging into his shoulders. He reached his hand between their bodies and rubbed her clit with his thumb. She moaned in pleasure and tightened her knees against his waist.

"Yes, yes, like that," she pleaded as she ground her pussy onto him.

"You want me?" He pushed deeper inside.

"I always want you. That's the problem because you always leave." Dammit. She didn't mean to say that now. She groaned. "Forget it."

"But I'm here now. Fuck. I know that sounds awful." He slowed his pace and touched her cheek with his fingers. "It's complicated for us, Jaida."

"Stop talking," she demanded as she slid his hand between her legs while she rocked on his cock. His thumb again found her tender and sensitive bud. Her excitement rose, her worries fled as pleasure gained control. By his rapid breathing she knew he was ready to explode.

If he kept touching her just that way, she would go over the edge too. Soon, very soon. The sensations coiled deep in her core and eased her up to find her peak. "Yes, oh yes."

Closing his eyes, he dropped his head back, as she felt his orgasm rack his body. "Jaida, I can't stop." The water splashed around them as he gripped the rocks from beneath and pumped into her until his seed spilled.

"It's okay, just don't slow down." She went quiet, her head down as she rocked on him with a sense of purpose.

He urged her on. "Oh yeah. Take it all."

She moved with fury, then a low groan escaped her lips. "Mmmm. Yes, I'm coming." Her body shook.

"Oh, yes. Come, baby," he said as he pulled her close.

Her breathing slowed. She rested her head on his chest. Goddess, she could fall in love with this man so easily. But it was such a bad idea. Doubt and frustration flashed in her thoughts again, her body stiffened. She turned in his arms, giving him a warning gaze. "Do me one favor."

His eyes widened. "What do you want?"

"When you leave Somerled, let me know ahead of time. Don't let me wake up and find out you've gone."

He hesitated. "Okay."

She narrowed her gaze then looked away. "I tossed the pebbles in the water and counted the ripples and asked my questions. The answers said—oh, never mind." He would leave without saying goodbye.

"More magic?"

Before she could answer, something wrapped around his neck and yanked him out of the pool.

CHAPTER 6

Green-eyed Dragon

Jaida screamed and was thrown to the side of the pool. Brayden's assailant dragged him over rough ground through the jungle. Naked, kicking and flailing his arms, Brayden struggled to stand and fight his enemy. He clawed at his throat, choking and gasping to breathe.

Branches scored his arms and legs as he was hauled along the trail.

"Stop it, you're choking him." Jaida yelled, but couldn't catch up. "Kai, stop!"

Finally, Brayden dug his fingers between his neck and Kai's slick tail and freed himself. He wrestled to his feet, spun around and glared at Kai. The dragon stood tall, wings beating furiously, green eyes glaring at Brayden defiantly. "What the fuck?" Brayden said hoarsely, rubbing his throat.

"Kai, what's the matter with you?" Jaida shouted as she caught up to them. Kai didn't bow his head as he did when he'd burned the lia-lia tree. With wings extended to their full length, he strutted passed Jaida and Brayden toward the coast.

"Is he getting an attitude or something?" Brayden asked.

"Or something," she commented. She had no idea how to explain Kai's true nature. As soon as they reached the coast, the secret would be out.

The sound of crashing waves and the scent of salty breezes sent Kai into a frenzy. Jaida grinned as she watched him charge through the flowering vines and palmettos, and over the powdery white sand dunes. He stopped before he reached the wet sand, pacing the water's edge of the sea-green ocean. There he glanced back as if waiting for her to join him.

"Not here, Kai," she warned. She laughed at his enthusiasm. Her belly twirled with anticipation at what would come and hoped she could keep Kai's secret from Brayden. If he was leaving like the pebbles told her, she decided Kai's nature must remain a secret.

"Is he afraid of the water?"

"No, he's definitely not afraid of the water. He'll go in later." But out of Brayden's sight. Then she would have lots to explain. She'd tell Brayden the same story she told the colonists.

"A dragon taking a swim in the ocean, should be quite a sight." Brayden turned his Comm-device over in his hand, and glanced at it.

"What are you doing?" She dropped her pack.

"Checking the weather. Looks good for a couple days."

"Good, we need to collect as much sargassia as we can and have Kai dry it." She ran into the water and scooped up handfuls of the greenish-brown lacy weed. The water was cool and refreshing. Brayden checked the sky, then removed his clothes and walked into the water to help her.

Hours later, sargassia hung over several vines staked to the ground or between palm trees. Kai inhaled and expelled streams of flames, igniting the drift wood beneath it, adding his heated breath to the kelp. The thin seaweed quickly dried and shriveled. Brayden and Jaida collected the paper-thin pieces into sacks.

"Can't you just dry the sargassia over an open fire without Kai?" Brayden tied off the last of the sacks.

"Kai's vapors are acidic which causes a chemical reaction in the sargassia. It makes the product more potent and stable."

"I see."

"It was fortunate I discovered the importance of the Dragon Tear Elixir before the colonists destroyed all the dragons. All but one, that is."

He nodded slowly. Jaida stretched out her bedroll while the remaining sargassia shriveled on the vines. Brayden unrolled his, sat beside her and studied his Comm-device.

"Checking the weather again?" she asked.

"Hmmm? No. Looks like there're a variety of fish in the ocean. Why don't the villagers come here to fish? It could supplement their food supply."

"Too long a trip."

He glanced up and down the beach. "Where's Kai?"

"Not far, he likes to explore, hunt for food. He'll be back soon."

Brayden continued to push buttons on his Comm. She pushed on his chest to make him lie down. "Stop your scientific studies for a moment. There's a naked woman within your grasp aching for your touch."

He hesitated a moment, then laughed and put his Comm-device away. Pulling her on top of him, his mouth took hers with such intensity, she gasped for breath. She barely took in another breath when strong human hands grabbed her from behind, lifted her off Brayden and carried her, racing toward the sea. Her cries were cut short when she gazed upon familiar green eyes. Brayden's angry shouts followed as he jumped up and charged after them. "It's okay, Brayden," she called back to him. He was still several paces behind. "Come out and join us."

"Jaida," Kai whispered with a sexy human voice, from a sexy human mouth.

Wrapping her arms around his neck, she speared her fingers into his long bronze hair. His tanned chest muscles and arms were slick with sea water. He stood about an inch or two taller than Brayden and had a leaner body. Her insides leapt for joy seeing his human form again after six long months.

How she missed him. She wanted to mate with him now. She wanted to mate with both men. She had to keep Kai's secret. Kai raced with her into the water, leaving Brayden behind looking stunned and angry.

"Trent, not Kai," her lovely dragon-man reminded her. When Kai was waist-deep, he slowly let her down onto her feet, still holding her in his arms and took her mouth in a bruising, heated kiss. The waves sloshed around them. She would have fallen had it not been for his body holding her. "Jaida." Kai saying her name sent a thrill through her.

"Kai, I mean Trent, you startled me." She laughed beneath his lips. "I need to explain to Brayden about you."

Trent's hands cradled and fondled her breasts, then slid down her belly, moving toward more intimate areas. The sound of splashing behind her brought her back to reality. Brayden.

"Hey," Brayden shouted. Trent abruptly stopped before his hand reached her mound and pierced her with his gaze. Stepping back into deeper water, he pulled her with him, then again embracing her.

"My thoughts vanish when I am in your arms, Jaida. The sea's power has freed me, yet this creature forgets to ask your permission to link."

Jaida pushed away from Trent. Walking into shallower water, she faced Brayden with a firm look. She held up her hand. "Brayden, stop. It's—"

"Let her go," Brayden demanded as he stormed toward them.

"Stop Bray-den, you do not want to war with me," Trent said. Brayden plowed through the waves and moved Jaida aside.

"The hell I don't."

She shoved back. "Brayden, he's a friend. This is Trent, he lives out here." She wouldn't give up Kai's secret that in his lifecycle, the sea water changed his race into human form for a brief time in order to mate. But since all the dragons were murdered as far as they knew, Kai had no one to mate with.

He would die without mating every six months even if the encounter didn't produce offspring. And it didn't. Their species weren't compatible.

"Yeah? I thought you said no one lives out here." Brayden said suspiciously.

Jaida crossed her arms over her bare breasts, the waves lapping at her pussy. "Except Trent. He likes his privacy. He had a disagreement with the colony and lives out here alone."

Brayden stared at Trent. "How do you survive?"

"I survive okay."

Jaida wondered if Brayden would ask about Trent's accent. He didn't sound like any of the colonists. Brayden slapped his arms at his sides and frowned. "You two are lovers?"

Trent smiled. Brayden sighed. "Okay, Jaida, Do you want me to…" he asked, hands on hips, his cock bobbing on the water.

Trent's mannerisms were a bit awkward in human form, but between his long bronze hair and searing green eyes, he was quite handsome—and more than capable as a lover—her gaze lowered to his aroused cock—and he was quite endowed.

As the waves surged over both men's engorged privates, swaying to the rhythms of the sea, Jaida couldn't help but smile, thinking what she could do.

"Jaida?" Brayden called impatiently. "Do you want to be alone with your friend? I'll take a walk."

"What I really want…" She touched Brayden's cheek and rubbed his shoulders, giving her support, but also stalling. The waves lapped at her body, the sensations stirring up desires like the anticipation of watching a coming storm. "Is to mate with him, Brayden, to be with both of you." She searched his face waiting for his response.

CHAPTER 7

Mating Ritual

Shadows of disappointment and conflicting emotions flashed across Brayden's face. His mouth twisted as if considering the offer. His eyes searched Jaida's face, then stared out to sea.

He didn't look angry, but he didn't look thrilled. Damn him. Why wouldn't he say something? She wasn't sure if he was angry, hurt or intrigued. After all, she was mating with an alien race, the last of his kind. Genetics wouldn't allow the mating to produce offspring. Their joining was for pleasure only, but for Trent's protection, she couldn't tell Brayden this.

"I'm sorry. I knew I should've told you before, but I was afraid you wouldn't agree to come. This has been our ritual for the past three years. The relationship Trent and I have is a…different kind, Brayden. It's hard to explain. I only see him twice a year."

Brayden nodded. "And where is Kai?"

She bit her lower lip, then said, "Enjoying his brief moments of freedom. The villagers don't like him running loose."

"I'll give you some privacy then." He turned and headed toward the shore, his shoulders slumped.

"Wait, Bray-den. You can share the joining," Trent said with the ease of a true free spirit. She covered her mouth as she giggled. Trent was full of surprises.

Brayden stopped and looked at Jaida for clarification. "Excuse me?" he asked.

Jaida grinned. "Trent wants you to participate if you'd like."

Brayden's eyes went wide. "In a threesome? That's what we're talking about?" He ran his hand through his hair, and pursed his lips, a look of doubt in his eyes.

"Jaida is a woman with enough light to share," Trent said holding his hand out to Brayden. Brayden glanced at Trent's hand then at Jaida.

"You said you wanted us both. I didn't think you meant at the same time. I have to think about this."

She moved closer, the tips of her nipples brushed his chest. Her mouth was teasingly close to his. "C'mon, Brayden. You can handle it." She slipped her hands up Brayden's chest and stood on tiptoes, crushing her mouth to his. He tasted of salt water. With her tongue, she probed into his mouth and heard a welcoming groan.

Brayden gripped her upper arms, drawing her close to keep her steady in the onslaught of waves. Both turned to see Trent smiling, bronze hair and bronze muscles gleaming wet from the sea, his body aroused and ready.

He took a few steps and, coming up behind Jaida, reached out and slid his hands around to cradle her breasts. She leaned back into him, jutting out her breasts as he tweaked the nipples almost painfully, sending zinging sensations straight to her groin.

"She is beautiful, is she not?" Trent asked Brayden.

Brayden nodded as he watched Kai fondle her. A thrill spun inside her gut as she enjoyed Brayden's stare and Trent's intimate touch. When Trent slid his hand down and probed her pussy, Brayden took his own cock in hand and began to stroke it.

"She is wet for us already. Here, feel her, Bray-den."

Brayden released himself and covered her mound, then slipped two fingers between her folds. Jaida widened her knees and leaned on Trent, gripping Brayden's shoulders for balance as he plunged his fingers inside. Leaning back exposed her clit for Trent's touch and Brayden's penetration. Two men pleasuring her pussy. Goddess, she was in heaven.

"A wildcat, isn't she?" Brayden asked Trent as he kissed her neck.

"Wildcat?" Trent looked confused.

"Wild and beautiful and dangerous." Brayden clarified.

"Yes, she is that."

Jaida moaned, then gripped Kai's legs. Her head rolled back on his shoulder, her body quivering.

"She's slick and hot inside," Brayden said as he rubbed her sensitive nub.

"Oh yes, she likes that, I remember," Trent said. "Take her, she's ready for you." Trent grasped Brayden's cock and directed it between her legs. Jaida felt Brayden's body stiffen and she noticed a frown of disapproval. "Crossed a boundary there?" she asked teasingly.

"Entering unknown territory, I'm afraid," Brayden answered without harsh tones.

Trent released Brayden's cock. "We shall not make a misadventure by offending each other. Forgive my intrusion," Trent said, green eyes intense as he stood back and lowered his head. Hard to look humble with a hard-on, but he did.

"No harm done." She grasped Brayden's cock that was thick and hard as she hooked one leg around his hip and guided his shaft between her legs. Trent's stiff erection slid between the cleft of her buttocks. His hands continued to palm and massage her breasts.

As Brayden pumped his cock into her the salt water made for some friction, but with Trent now rubbing her clit her juices quickly flowed. Between Trent supporting her from behind and her one leg around Brayden's hip, Jaida barely stood in the water on her own.

One good strong wave and the three of them would tumble over in a heap. Trent's tongue stroked the side of her neck, and he whispered in her ear. "Who do you think will make you come?"

The warm breath of his husky words sent a shiver down her back, encouraging Brayden to deepen his thrusts. "Don't even try to make this a competition," she demanded. "It'll take all the fun out of it."

All resistance appeared to be gone now from Brayden's face. She was surprised how perfectly this encounter had worked out, a sexual fantasy come true. As long as Brayden didn't find out who Trent truly was.

Brayden grabbed her ass and began to pump hard and fast. Trent braced her shoulders so she felt the full impact of the thrusts. Then Brayden slowed his pace and pulled out, gasping for breath. "I'd like this to last."

"Shall we continue on the beach?" Trent asked.

"Mmmm. That works for me. How about you, Jaida?" Brayden bent and sucked her nipples.

Trent's finger teased the sensitive skin around her anus, testing for access. "I think she could take us both."

Brayden raised an eyebrow, but spoke no words.

She was about to say she wasn't sure how she felt about the idea, when Brayden slid a finger inside her pussy and rubbed her clit with his thumb. "You two are going to drive me mad. I'm ready for the beach."

Brayden swept her up in his arms and glanced at Trent. "Let's go, Trent. Time's a wasting." He carried her to shore and tumbled onto the bedrolls, Jaida alongside him, while Trent dropped down at her feet and spread her legs.

Brayden knelt beside Jaida as if uncertain what to do next. She took his cock in her hand and stroked it. "Are you coming back inside me?"

"If you like. But we're sharing." He looked at Trent. There was something not right about the guy, but he couldn't figure it out. Jaida had been seeing him for years. He was suddenly jealous of that time. Out of the water, Trent look tired, his face drained. "Do you need to rest?" Brayden asked.

Maybe the guy didn't get enough food out here. Kneeling between Jaida's legs, Trent's fingers spread her folds exposing her sensitive and engorged bud. He rubbed it gently with his thumb and she moaned and raised her hips. "I am fine. I have until I am finished with this, finished mating. Do not be concerned." He bent over and lapped at her clit and Jaida cried out, gripping Brayden's cock a little too tightly.

"Easy wildcat. I'd like to use that again." That was the second time Trent called it mating, not sex, making love or even fucking. Odd.

She giggled. "Oh, sorry. Straddle me. I want to suck you off," she said to Brayden.

"Okay, be gentle though," Brayden teased as he swung his leg over her chest, his knees on either side of her shoulders. She took him in her mouth and cupped his balls. He supported her head between his hands as he gently rocked his hips, then she grasped his shaft and stroked it up and down while she slid her mouth on him and teased the tip with her tongue.

Oh yeah, he was done for. With her moans and the thought of Trent licking her pussy it didn't take him long to be thrust over the precipice as the orgasm slammed into his body. He heard a murmur of approval from Trent and his body shook as Jaida held him in her mouth until he was spent.

Finally, his knees shaking, he slid from her and dropped at her side. At that moment Trent entered her pussy. Inside Brayden's backpack his Comm-device signaled with a beep. He rolled away from the couple and reached for the electronic unit and pressed the key to "acknowledge receipt of message" but left it in his pack.

The ship would arrive tomorrow. He didn't have much time. He slipped on his pants and sat back down on the bedroll, keeping his eyes on Trent. The beach bum had finished and lay beside her, twisting Jaida's hair between his fingers. Maybe that's all Trent was, a beach bum. No harm in that.

They didn't seem to notice that Brayden was partially dressed. He needed to go find the dragon. Trent pushed up on one elbow, facing Brayden, but his full attention was on Jaida. He began to fondle her breasts. A twinge of jealousy stung Brayden, a foolish thought considering what they had just done. With one finger, Brayden drew lazy patterns on her shoulder, down her arm to her hip.

She turned and smiled at him briefly and squeezed his hand, then returned her gaze to Trent. The beach bum's long bronze hair hung in his eyes. "Our time, Jaida, is always too brief, much too brief, but wondrous just the same."

Feeling like he was intruding on their moment, Brayden got up. "I'll be right back."

"Mother nature call?" Jaida asked.

He nodded. "Won't be long."

"It's getting dark. Don't go too far." She smiled sadly at Trent. "Trent, stay here for the night."

"But the morning…" he argued.

"I know. Stay anyway," Jaida said. "It'll be all right." Jaida had her back to Brayden and didn't realize he was still standing there.

Trent glanced at Brayden as if giving him a pleading look, perhaps looking for approval. Why did Trent need to ask permission to sleep with them? Brayden smiled and nodded anyway. Between the sex and the messages to the ship, he'd been so busy he hadn't asked where Trent lived or how he managed to survive out here.

Trent smiled back at Brayden. Guilt consumed him for what he was about to do. He tasted bile at the back of his throat. He turned and walked down the beach looking for the dragon. If only there was another way.

CHAPTER 8

Captured

That night the three of them briefly slept in each other's arms, Jaida between her two men while warm ocean breezes stroked their skin. A couple of hours after their last heated encounter, Braden was awakened by the grunts and deep breathing of two people in the throes of sex.

Still half asleep, he forced his eyes open and stared blankly at the glittering stars through the palm trees. Was the commander's ship up there orbiting Somerled? At first light, he'd have to go in search of the dragon again.

His body felt twice as heavy from the grogginess of sleep. He blinked several times trying to wake up, then felt someone sucking his cock. He looked down and was grateful to see it was Jaida. He understood that it was possible in a threesome arrangement that Trent could accidentally touch him intimately, or he could brush up against Trent. He didn't have a problem with that, but he wasn't crazy about the idea of Trent sucking him off. Some boundaries he wasn't ready to cross yet.

She was kneeling between his legs, her fist wrapped tight around the base of his shaft as her mouth took him in deep and her tongue swirled the head. He groaned and dug his fingers into the blankets. "Damn, Jaida, slow down or I'm going to come."

She hummed her approval but didn't let up. He lifted his head and saw that Trent was behind her, his hands gripping her ass as he pumped into her. Trent's eyes met his. The emotion he saw was intense, pure anger. Was it a trick of the darkness? Or was it really anger?

Trent slammed into Jaida even harder as she moaned against Brayden's cock, gripping his shaft firmly. The sight and sensations sent Brayden over the edge. Then Trent pulled her off him and turned her over onto her back beside Brayden and entered her again.

Jaida reached her hand out to Brayden, stroking his chest. His cock still throbbed while watching the two in their passionate embrace. He held her hand while Trent made love to her. Trent glanced up and scowled at Brayden. Rage gleamed in his eyes. What was up with this guy? Trent was the free spirit. What's with the attitude? He let go of her hand, suddenly feeling like the intruder.

Jaida screamed and thrashed her body as her orgasm consumed her. Closing his eyes, Trent grasped her breasts, and rocked his hips, then cried out as his body shuddered and reached his climax. He froze there for a moment then gathered Jaida in his arms, holding her possessively to his chest, both breathing heavy.

"Brayden, join us," Jaida said as she reached for his hand. Reluctantly, Brayden knelt behind her, stroking her shoulders and back, kissing her neck and hair.

"Jaida, let's go for a swim." Trent scooped her up. Jaida giggled with delight as Trent raced across the dark beach.

"Jaida, are you all right?" Brayden called after them.

"Sure, we'll be right back," she called, giggling some more, then he heard a splash and more giggles. He saw the silhouettes of two people embracing. A twinge of jealously dug into him. They've been together for three years. He would consider challenging that, being the man in her life if he didn't have his mission to complete. But in a few hours Jaida would hate him. Brayden closed his eyes and cursed the situation. He leaned back on the blanket where she had slept and breathed in her scent.

Never had Jaida felt such joy. Never had she imagined she would experience this type of erotic pleasure with two men. She loved them both for different reasons. Kai for his companionship, his kindness and free spirit. Brayden for his strength, his honesty and sense of adventure, even though she knew it meant he would leave her again.

She was convinced he felt something for her. She saw the longing in his eyes. Perhaps, he'd try to see her again between flights. She'd accept the moments they would have, however brief.

In chest-high water, Kai held her in his arms and slowly spun her around without a word. "What is it, Kai? You seemed angry before and now distant."

"Bray-den will leave soon. He will hurt you."

"I know. He can't stay. He's a pilot and he'll have to return to his ship."

"It will be soon."

"How do you know?"

"I sense it." Kai was sensitive to her feelings, though he never said he could read minds. She stroked his skin. The bronze smoothness was beginning to feel rough, a sign that his scales would be returning soon. His twenty-four hours as a human were almost over. Soon, even the sea wouldn't revive him. Kai would reform into the dragon phase for another six months. Tears burned in her eyes. "Do not be sad, Jaida. What happens is what should be." She forced a smile and held him close as the warm waves caressed them.

* * *

Brayden woke to a brilliant orange sunrise, something he never saw out in space. Trent and Jaida were asleep, a tangle of arms and legs beside him. They looked like two shipwrecked lovers on a deserted island. Sitting up, Brayden searched up and down the beach for the dragon. Damn, he was going to be in a lot of trouble if the ship arrived and there was no dragon.

The Comm-device signaled with a consistent beep. He cringed when the noise woke Trent. He stretched and looked at Brayden. The man did not look well. His skin had lost its bronze color and looked more grayish. His green eyes had a dull appearance too.

"Are you feeling okay, Trent?"

Trent nodded and stood, taking in a deep breath. He didn't take his eyes off Brayden. Then his skin and body began to change. His skin took on the appearance of reptilian scales. Trent's arms shifted, stretched, leathery webs grew between rib cage and arms. His torso took on a denser shape, that of the dragon.

A sound came from Brayden, part shock, part agony as if he felt Trent's pain and realized the creature he was going to abduct was Trent. The ultimate betrayal. "Kai, no," Jaida sat up, glancing at Brayden. "Brayden, you can't tell. Kai would be in danger. Promise you won't tell."

He didn't answer but turned to watch Trent continue in his transformation, while Brayden's heart ripped in half. Taking a few steps back, Trent glanced at Jaida with a bittersweet smile. The sadness in his eyes stabbed at

Brayden's chest. It must be like a man going back to prison. Jaida stood and pulled on her sarong.

Tears glistened in her eyes as she watched Kai finish the change. Trent's fingers lengthened into talons, clawing at the air, testing their new form while flames spewed from his mouth. His legs and feet were now that of the dragon. No sign of the man remained.

Kai beat his wings, then roared. Triumphant? Gratified? Frustrated? Brayden didn't know, but the dragon appeared quite pleased and content. Strong and vital again. The creature was an enigma. "What's that noise, Brayden?" she asked.

"Getting a call. They can leave a message." He picked up the Comm-device and pressed a few keys to initiate the homing signal.

"Who's calling?"

"I'll check later."

"He's beautiful, isn't he?" Her voice cracked. Brayden kissed her hair.

"Now, I understand why you've been protecting him. I love you, Jaida."

She pushed out of his embrace and stared at him, a hint of a curve twitched at one side of her mouth. She sighed. "Brayden, why would you say that when you will never stay?"

"It's true. No matter our differences or what happens. And I see how special Kai is."

"Yes, Kai is special. And now that you understand how special, you must help me protect him. He's the last of his kind. I can tell you that he does nothing to enhance the Dragon Tear Elixir."

Brayden blinked. "What?"

"The Elixir is nothing more than nutrients—much needed nutrients considering the colonists' diet, but supplements just the same. Kai adds nothing, but it's my way of protecting him."

Brayden drove his hand through his hair. "Like the traveling salesmen of the Old West selling health tonics that were worthless?"

"Dragon Tears Elixir is not worthless," she argued, then turned to see Kai as his body finished the transformation. Hands to her mouth, Jaida's eyes filled with tears. Brayden rapidly punched additional coordinates into his Comm-device and prepared for what he was about to do, what he already regretted having to do. How much would Kai remember in his magical form? Would he remember the betrayal?

The dragon's roar was masked by the thundering roar of shuttle engines.

CHAPTER 9

Planetside Peril

J aida raced out to the middle of the beach, and Kai
ran toward the shuttle the moment it landed,
flapping his wings, spitting flames and smoke.
Brayden thought the dragon was going to attack it like
another beast.

"Kai, stop," Jaida cried.

Brayden raced after him and tossed a flat disk with a
flick of his wrist. The crystalline restraint unwound as it
shot through the air and dropped over Kai like a fine-
meshed netting that instantly hardened on contact. Kai
roared and struggled, captive and immobile beneath the
net. Even puffs of smoke and flames could not penetrate
it.

Jaida screamed. "Brayden, stop. What are you doing?"
She ran to Kai and yanked on the prison, but Brayden
stopped her. The hatred in her eyes crushed him, equaling
the moment when he'd learned that his father's ship had

crashed. Brayden wasn't a daredevil like his dad, but Brayden had made a huge mistake by giving in to the politics of the Fleet and bringing those thirty people to an unstable and dangerous planet.

Right now he would do anything to take that pain away from Jaida's eyes, remove the hatred he saw there, but he would not sacrifice thirty lives.

"I have to, Jaida, and I can't explain why. I'm following orders. I have no choice." Four men in Fleet uniforms jumped out of the shuttle and raced over to Kai. Moments later, they loaded him into a hovering crate and dragged it toward the shuttle.

Jaida ran after them. "He's the last of his kind. He's not a creature, you idiots, he's sentient. Stop!"

Ignoring her, one of the men in the same black uniform that Brayden wore shouted, "Let's roll, Brayden."

"I'm ready." He gave Jaida one last look. Angry tears stained her cheeks. He knew reaching out to her would be useless. "I'm sorry, Jaida. I had no choice."

She glared at him in a mixture of horror and sadness beyond anything he could comprehend. "I never saw this side of you, Brayden. Maybe you weren't capable of loving me, but I didn't think you were capable of evil. You bastard, you have him trapped like an animal." She punched his chest, then ran after the men who were taking the carrier with Kai up the ramp. They pushed her roughly away.

Brayden ran over and knocked the guy off his feet. "I told you not to hurt her. Get the fuck inside. I'll take care of this."

"Yes, sir." Red-faced, the man turned and marched up the ramp.

Brayden noticed that Kai had never taken his eyes off her. The dragon couldn't struggle beneath the restraint net, or they never would've gotten him on board. The men disappeared with Kai into the ship. Brayden stood at the top of the ramp. "I'm sorry, Jaida. If there was another way—"

"Stokes! Gotta go now." One of the men called from inside. Jaida stood, arms crossed, tears streaming down her face as her body shook in racking sobs. And it was his fault. He had never navigated around a black hole as vast as the crushing one in his chest right now.

CHAPTER 10

Dragon Flame

When the shuttle docked within the *Valafar*, crewmen rolled Kai's crated prison onto the ship. The look of hatred and betrayal from the dragon singed Brayden's soul. He leaned down close and whispered, "I promise somehow, someday, I'll make this up to you, Kai."

Kai didn't move or acknowledge him. "Well, I have to say, Captain Stokes, I'm impressed." Commander Krentz smacked Brayden on the shoulder. "This will round out my collection of exotic wildlife quite nicely."

"You're keeping him onboard?" Brayden feared what the commander might have in mind.

"For now, until I get an offer I can't refuse. But I must have a gala to show him off." He pointed to one of the guards. "You get him in his display and make sure his muzzle is on. We don't need him burning up the inside of the *Valafar*."

"Yes, commander." The guard rolled Kai away. There was nothing Brayden could do right now.

"My payment, sir." Brayden couldn't waste another moment.

"Still determined to save those colonists?"

"I need a few crew members, food, emergency—"

"Yes, yes, your ship is ready. Here." Krentz handed him his papers. You're to relocate the colony on Calibor, if you're in time.

* * *

Several weeks after Brayden rescued and relocated the colonist from Krakatan, he returned to the *Valafar* and descended to the lower engine levels where the animal enclosures held Kai. The dragon wouldn't even look at him.

Brayden couldn't steal him. Even if he did, Krentz would know where to find him and the dragon. Theft would be considered piracy, and he'd walk a plank into the vacuum of space. Not the best way to help Kai. But he did have another idea to get Kai back to Somerled.

In the crew's lounge, Krentz held up the empty bottle of Cahoon Jack and gave Rhosyn, the young woman crew member, a questioning look. "Rhosyn, we're dry again."

"Not a problem." She got up, glancing at Brayden as she walked over to the walled storage compartments. Returning with a fresh bottle, she poured Krentz a full glass. Krentz had nearly cleaned him out of his last four months of credits in Robard's Bluff. He couldn't decipher any tells from Krentz, but he was beginning to figure out tells from his woman. Was Rhosyn trying to help him? If she was, and she was caught, she'd get in a lot of trouble.

"Hey, woman, you're hurting me," Krentz complained as she poured him another glass of the alcohol.

"You can handle it," she answered. "Anyone else?" She held up the bottle. One crew member raised his glass. Brayden and the other young recruit drank bottled beer.

"I'm good," Brayden said. The commander won that hand and Brayden was worried because he might run out of credits before he could win Kai. Krentz could get drunk and still beat most men at Robard's Bluff. Hell, half conscious he could win.

Brayden was screwed. He had his pilot's license, but Kai was imprisoned like an animal. Rhosyn gave him a knowing look at his chips then at the pot. Was she telling him to bet more? He decided to take the chance. He placed a stack into the pot.

"A bold move, Stokes," Krentz said. "You're going to lose your license again."

"Perhaps." The commander raised his bid and Brayden matched it. Two more players dropped out. The hand was turned over and Brayden won.

"Fuck you, Stokes. Since when do you get smart at cards?"

"Just lucky." His luck had better hold out. The next hand, Rhosyn bit her lip. Brayden bid light.

"What's the matter, Stokes, lose your nerve?" Another crew member dropped out. Brayden lost that hand. Dammit, she is helping me. Another couple of hands, and Brayden picked up a few more tells from Rhosyn. The woman opened a few buttons on her shirt then stroked Krentz's leg. The commander pushed her hand away.

"Is there a story behind Robard's Bluff?" Rhosyn asked as she poured more CJ into the commander's glass. What was she up to? Trying to distract Krentz? Get him drunk? Nice, sweetheart. But she should know the commander could play just as well drunk or sober. They were better off, hitting him now while they had a little communication going, before Krentz caught on.

"Yes, there is a story behind Robard's Bluff," Brayden said. "I'll tell you about it another time."

Rhosyn gave Brayden a worried look, then seemed to catch on. "Oh yes, I'd love to hear it."

"Another time, darling," Krentz said as he dealt out another hand. She slipped her hand on his lap and Brayden figured she was stroking his cock. Krentz smiled but shoved her hand aside. "Let me finish this game and we'll fuck." She nodded.

Stay cool, Brayden thought. She actually gave Krentz a little pout. Brayden managed not to laugh. She leaned back and glanced at Krentz's cards while he sipped his drink and sighed. She bit her lip. Brayden bid light and lost. On the next hand, Rhosyn's eyes widened and glanced at Brayden's stack of chips and then at the pot. This was it, his chance. Now or never. "I think we should make this hand interesting," Brayden said.

"About time," Krentz said. "What do you have in mind?" Krentz folded his cards in his hand, laid them flat on the table and kept his eyes on Brayden. She smiled and refilled his glass with the CJ. Good girl. "Put the fucking bottle down," Krentz said.

Rhosyn did what she was told without flinching. She knew exactly what she was doing. She was trying to distract him. "You wouldn't be helping him, would you?" Krentz asked. She glared at him.

"I don't even know how to play."

Krentz laughed. "This is true. I've tried teaching her a few times. She's smart when it comes to electronics, but clueless when it comes to playing cards." The room filled with a heavy silence.

Brayden poured himself a CJ in an empty glass on the table. He took a swig. The sweet amber liquid burned at the back of his throat.

"Robard was a space pirate in the Outer Rim," Krentz began. "He'd hang out in the traffic zones and play possum until a transport ship came through to investigate the disabled ship. Back then, transport ships weren't heavily armed. Easy prey. Robard would take their goods, sometimes their women. Fleet security finally caught up with him," Krentz told Rhosyn but kept his eyes on Brayden.

The commander studied him with suspicious eyes. "They armed a small transport vessel and when Robard tried to trap them with his disabled ship routine, they arrested him. But there is no judge or jury for pirates. They made him walk the plank into the vacuum of space as an example to any other space pirates."

Rhosyn stared wide-eyed with amusement. "Wow. I've not heard of any pirates since I joined the Fleet."

"That's the basis of this game, my dear."

"Interesting, maybe I'll learn one of these days." She smiled at him as if she'd forgotten his rudeness earlier.

"All right, Stokes. Tell me your interesting bet."

Brayden's head began to pound. This had to work or Kai would remain in Krentz's strange and bizarre creature feature, Brayden would lose his pilot's license again and Jaida would never talk to him, would probably kill him if she ever saw him again. Terrific.

"Just you and me, Stokes," Krentz said. "Are you going to bet or daydream?"

Brayden studied his hand, then glanced at Krentz. He hoped Rhosyn was right or he was screwed. "I'll bet my pilot's license." Bile slid up Brayden's throat.

Krentz laughed and pounded his fist. "You're a fucking fool. And what am I supposed to bet?" Krentz pressed his lips together as he leaned forward.

"The dragon."

Krentz's mouth dropped open. "No, goddamn way. Forget it."

"Okay, then I'll take the *Zepar* out of here tonight. Not sure when I'll be back. Rescuing those colonists got back to Fleet. They were very pleased, and I hear I may get transferred to another unit. Of course, if I'm in another unit, I won't be available to barter any goods for you. And I did make you quite a wealthy man."

Krentz's fingers drummed the table as he was considering Brayden's words. Brayden continued. "I'll add to my bet. Besides the pilot's license for the dragon, I'd also agree not to accept a transfer to another unit within the Fleet." Rhosyn stroked Krentz's back and Brayden saw the man's face turn red. The commander shoved Rhosyn away.

"Fine. I'll take the bet." Krentz stared at his cards and frowned, the first time Brayden had seen him give an expression away during a card game. "Stop stalling, Stokes. Turn the fucking cards over." Brayden spread his cards out without emotion on his face and held his breath. Studying the cards for a couple seconds, Krentz grimaced.

Shit. Rhosyn was wrong. He glanced at her and saw her smile. She betrayed him. She was loyal to Krentz all along. How did he get himself roped into this? Krentz tossed his cards down.

"Fuck you, Stokes. Get your ass and dragon off my vessel," Krentz said through clenched teeth. "By the way, you're fired." Rhosyn pursed her lips together, as if holding back a smile. She glanced at Brayden for only a second. But the message was clear. "Way to go."

* * *

"We're running low on the Dragon Tear Elixir, Jaida," Mr. Moretti said as he stood in her kitchen and loaded his knapsack with teas, powders and other apothecary wares. "Many villagers are planning to leave Somerled because of the toxic atmosphere. Without the Elixir…"

"The villagers don't have to leave," Jaida said. She'd waited long enough. It was two months since Kai was taken and the pain hadn't eased, but she had to tell the colonists the truth about the Dragon Tear Elixir and hope they could forgive her.

"They don't want to take the risk." He continued to load his supplies.

"But there is no risk."

He dropped his knapsack and narrowed his eyes. "You found another way to make the Elixir?"

She shook her head. "I hope you'll understand… The sargassia kelp does not need to be dried with the dragon's flame."

"But Jaida, how will—"

"I know what I said. It's not true. I said that only to protect Kai, but he's gone now so it doesn't matter. And the Elixir is not needed to detox the effects of the atmosphere. The atmosphere is fine, I falsified my studies. I lied, I'm sorry."

"The Dragon Tear Elixir is worthless?" His shoulders slumped. He looked more hurt than angry and that was what upset Jaida the most.

"No. It is valuable to help maintain good health with our limited diet, but not life and death as I made you believe." Mr. Moretti frowned. She was afraid he'd leave his supplies and she would be ostracized from the colony.

"Why, dear?" he said softly. "Just to save the dragon?"

She shook her head. "And me. Every planet I've been to, I've lost loved ones. First my brother, then my parents disowned me. Kai was like family, you all are my family now. I had to do something to prove that I was important for the survival of the colony, not just a woman who grew medicinal herbs and worked a little magick."

Mr. Moretti chuckled and hugged her like a father would his daughter. "Easy, my dear. All are necessary for the survival of the colony. I see you are growing new plants in your garden. Food or herbs?" He brushed her tears away as he held her at arm's length.

"Both. I've traveled into the mountains and found new varieties."

"And we'll keep the Elixir our little secret. I'll tell them you discovered something you can mix with it instead." He winked at her, then picked up his knapsack. "Wouldn't want to lower your prices, now, or my percentage." He hurried outside, and she watched him ascend the path to town.

Somehow, she had the feeling he was being protective of her. Using the minimal profit he made as an excuse to keep her deception a secret. Some colonists might not be as forgiving. The smell of burning wood wafted into her open door, then the sound of crackling flames. No! Not her garden. It was the dry season. A bushfire? She ran outside.

Standing in her garden, she saw Kai beside her lia-lia tree. But the tree wasn't on fire. Brayden stood beside Kai with a huge grin, holding a burning branch. He waved the branch like a flag then tossed it into a bucket of water to douse the flames. The dragon beat his wings, then drew them to his body and sat on his haunches and bowed his head. "Hello, Jaida," Brayden said, a pleased smile on his face.

"You bastard. What are you doing here?"

She raced over and pummeled him in the chest. He took a step back and tried to grab her arms. "Hold on."

She punched and slapped and aimed for his head. "Son of bitch."

Raising his arms, he blocked most of the blows. "Easy, easy. I needed to trade a dragon for my license so I could rescue some colonists on a planet before it became a volcanic catastrophe." She stopped her attack for a moment to listen. "Everyone survived, by the way," he added.

"You sold my dragon!" She slapped him.

"Ow! No, borrowed your dragon. I brought him back." He rubbed his cheek.

She poked him in the chest. "You could've asked."

He took her hand to halt the pokes. "Couldn't risk you saying no. I saved thirty lives. I think that makes me a hero." He wagged his eyebrows.

She tapped her foot on the ground. "When are you leaving this time? Soon I hope."

"Sorry you said that, because I've lost my license again." One side of his mouth slid up to a grin.

"Again? Yeah right."

She turned and went inside her house and slammed her door. A blast of heat emanated from the other side. She opened the door to find Kai glaring at her. Kai was standing up for Brayden? Very odd. Brayden leaned against the side of the house and shot her a smart-ass look. "He understands why I had to do it."

"To save lives," she said. "And how did you get Kai back?"

"Won him in a lucky hand of Robard's Bluff."

"You gambled on my—"

"Dragon?" Brayden finished. "Yep. And my commander honors his gambling debts, but didn't see a reason to keep me employed. I've lost my Fleet license for good. So I'm stuck here. I've had enough of the corrupt lifestyle of a Fleet pilot. I'm going to learn to fly as a dragon pilot and be a farmer." He smirked.

Jaida giggled, crossing her arms. "If you stay, I can't wait to see you knee-deep in the rice paddies."

"I'll stay if you'll have me. Or take the next shuttle out. Find another planet," Brayden said huskily. "Just say the word."

"You really are staying."

He nodded and pulled her in for a demanding and sensuous kiss, one she felt to the tip of her toes. She took a few breaths and smiled. Oh, the magick she would work with Brayden planetside.

"In about four months, we'll be taking our excursions to the sea with Kai." Brayden smiled at Jaida. Her stomach fluttered with anticipation of the three of them making love by the sea again. Jaida turned and walked back inside. Looking over her shoulder, she gave Brayden a sultry smile. "Are you coming?"

"In a minute. After I go out for a spin around the village. I haven't given up flying, just my mode of transportation." Brayden climbed onto Kai's back and with several beats of his wings, Kai leapt off the ground and soared toward the village.

THE END

GLOSSARY

Aquasam – A type of ointment that Jaida makes for the colonists on Somerled for moisturizing and eliminating pain.

Cahoon Jack – An alcoholic beverage, quite strong.

Comm-device – A portable communication device for Fleet crewman.

Current Laws and Customs Data Sheets – Detailed information about a planet given to colonists when they settle to help them acclimate. It's also to warn them of other wildlife and sentient beings who may inhabit the planet.

Dragon Tear Elixir – A lotion made from sargassia seaweed and cured by a dragon's flame. The colonists need this for survival on Somerled to protect them from toxic elements in the atmosphere. Most colonists believe it also has aphrodisiac properties.

Fleet Exploration Organization – Federal organization in charge of discovering new humanoid inhabitable planets and providing transfer of colonists and supplies. The farther out in space, the more corrupt with black market trading.

Krakatan – A planet with new colonists. The planet was never approved as safe and is now unstable with life-threatening volcanic activity.

Lialia – A type of tree with citrus-like fruit.

Mandara – The previous planet where Jaida lived. Not good memories.

Outer Rim – An area of the galaxy considered the new frontier of space.

Robard's Bluff – A card game played on the ships, usually a gambling game.

Sargassia – A seaweed found on Somerled used to make a special elixir that protects the colonist from toxic elements in the atmosphere.

Shapeshifter – A being or person who can change their physical form. The change may occur at will or be initiated by an external source like moonlight, or as in Dragon Witch, by seawater.

Somerled – The new planet settlement where Jaida lives. Dragons once lived there. All are thought to have been destroyed except one—Kai.

Valafar – The large ship that Brayden is stationed on.

Zapar – Brayden's personal ship used for transporting colonists and supplies.

ABOUT KATHY

New York Times & *USA Today* bestselling author Kathy Kulig is known for her sexy paranormal and contemporary romances that are passionate, intense and riveting. These emotionally-charged stories are full of heart and always have a happy ending.

She began her writing career in journalism, publishing articles in magazines and newspapers. Kathy has been featured or quoted in the *Chicago Tribune, Writer's Digest, Romantic Times Magazine, USA Today* HEA, *Bustle Magazine, Florida Weekly,* and appeared on several radio shows. She has spoken at national and local conferences, writer's groups and libraries.

When she's not writing, she loves to work out, travel, read good books, watch movies and have dinners out with her darling husband. She lives in Pennsylvania in a 100-year-old Victorian house with a garage built out of reject tombstones.

Connect with Kathy on her website: www.kathykulig.com. Subscribe to her newsletter so you don't miss a thing! Read more about Kathy, her books, contest and upcoming projects by subscribing to her mailing list. http://smarturl.it/KathysHotNews

A Note from the Author

THANK YOU FOR READING!

I hope you enjoyed reading this book as much as I enjoyed writing it. I grew up reading science fiction and paranormal books, and watching television shows like Twilight Zone, Outer Limits and Night Gallery. Okay, I may be dating myself, but I loved these series, and my bookshelves started filling up with supernatural books at an early age.

These shows featured thought–provoking dark fantasy, science fiction and supernatural stories. All were stand alone. By the way, Night Gallery featured the directorial debut Steven Spielberg!

ABOUT DARK REALMS SERIES

Influenced by these television shows, and my love for paranormal and speculative fiction, I've created the Dark Realms series. It's is a collection of sensual romance novellas and short novels with supernatural heroes and fantasy, science fiction or paranormal elements. Shifters, witches, vampires, ghosts and more. These stories can be set on Earth, on other planets, within another dimension or time. You'll find supernatural heroes who haunt us, hunt us and hunger passionately for us. Each book is a complete and individual story. No cliffhangers!

The books can be read in any order.

Reviews are helpful to authors. I really appreciate all reviews, both positive and negative. If you want to leave one, please do so on Goodreads or your favorite retailer! If you liked this story, you might also enjoy other books in the Dark Realms series as well as other books by Kathy Kulig. Visit her website www.kathykulig.com.

Preview
Edge of Passion

CHAPTER 1

“The park's closed today,” the gray-haired gentleman at the visitor's desk said in a slow Irish drawl. He scowled at his computer screen then scribbled notes on a piece of paper without looking at her.

“I'm not a tourist, I'm Dana Brennan. I was hired as a musician for the show.”

Glancing up from his work, he gave her a quick once-over and frowned. “What happened to you, miss? You're soaking wet.” He stood and approached the counter from the other side, giving her a closer look. “Didn't fall into the bog now, did you?”

“Bog? No, I had a flat tire on my drive over. It was raining.”

“Changed it yourself now?”

She nodded.

He smiled, clearly astonished. He was a man of indeterminate years with white hair, a weatherworn face and blue eyes that held humor one moment, and severity the next.

"I'll get you your key so you can get into dry clothes. I'm Will Donegal, the proprietor of Rathmoor Castle." He opened several drawers until he held up a key. "Here you go, Ms. Brennan. Take the road to the right of the castle. You'll find the cottages for the performers." He handed her the key with the number six on it. "You be an American? First time in Ireland?"

"I am American, but I've visited before. My cousin lives in Dublin. She told me about the job."

"I'd come and show you the cottage, but I best be staying here. Being it's Monday, the park is closed, but tourists still wander in."

Her spirits fell. "Darn. I was hoping to check out the castle. It looks magnificent from the outside."

"It is that now, isn't it?" His eyes brightened and his back straightened, then he turned serious again. "You'll have plenty of time to explore the castle when it's open."

"I will. Thanks." She sighed. "I'm supposed to meet Jack. I understand he's the one who hired me." They'd talked on the phone and emailed for months. She had all the music he'd sent her memorized for the show. She couldn't wait to meet him. Curiosity stirred that fluttery sensation in her stomach.

She couldn't help but wonder if his looks matched her fantasy image of him. At the same time, she worried if she didn't perform well, Jack had the power to fire her, and this exciting summer job and vacation would abruptly end.

His voice had a slow, rugged sound. Maybe it was the Irish accent or her pitiful love life that had kicked her libido into gear. She hadn't had anything more than a casual date over the last six months. Knowing her luck, Jack probably looked more like the proprietor.

"Jack's around," Mr. Donegal said. "His cottage is at the edge of the forest, number two. And best you don't wander into that forest alone. You could get lost in the bogs."

"I'll keep that in mind." Get lost? She used to go backpacking in the Shenandoah National Park alone and she never got lost. She thought better not to mention that. "I had a large package shipped. Do you know if it's arrived yet?"

He pondered her question for a moment. "Yes, it's here. Delivered two days ago."

"Where is it? How did it look?" She clasped her hands to her chest, preparing herself for the worse.

He gave her a puzzled look. "Why, it looked like a box, a rather large one at that."

"I mean was it damaged?

"Don't think so."

"Good. Can I pick it up now, please?"

"Jack took it. Said it was your harp. Probably took it to the castle for the show."

"And the castle is closed," she reminded him. Her heart leapt with relief and disappointment. By the look on the proprietor's face, he wasn't going to leave his post so she could get her instrument.

"Ah, I love the folk harp. 'Tis a lovely sound. I shall look forward to hearing you play."

"Thank you, Mr. Donegal."

He caught her gaze and gave her a slight nod. "If you follow the drive, you'll come to a fork. Bear to the right. You'll see the cottages. There's a meeting tonight at seven in the castle for the entertainers. You can get your harp then."

She thanked him again and left the visitor's center with its quaint thatched roof and miniature windows with flower boxes, like something straight out of a fairytale. Despite her disappointment in having to wait to practice her music, her summer job excited her. Her parents had frowned on Dana's decision to take a leave of absence from a well-paying management position in a security company for this part-time, minimal-paying job as an entertainer in a medieval show.

Both high-powered executives, they thrived on long work hours and stress. How could they understand that the stress of Dana's job had been wearing on her life?

Work usually slowed down in her company over the summer, so her boss had agreed to the leave as long as she returned by September first. She deserved this break. At thirty-three, this was the first reckless thing she'd ever done.

The midday sun dried the earlier rain and the air smelled of dew, cut grass and flowers. For a Maryland girl, June in Ireland was on the cool side. She climbed into her rental car, which looked more like a fishbowl on a roller skate, and drove along the gravel road toward Rathmoor Castle. As she reached the fork in the road, she stopped the car. Across a large field toward the right, a dozen thatched-roofed cottages lined the edge of a dense forest. The left fork led straight to the castle. The ancient castle stood in the center of a large meadow. The worn stone edifice conveyed power and strength. The centuries hadn't diminished that.

As she gazed at the massive structure, a slight tremor went through her. Mostly, she shivered from cold. The rain had soaked through to her underwear and the cool air had chilled her to the bone. But the tremor was more than that. She couldn't imagine her good luck at working in such a beautiful place, but what if her parents were right and taking this time off would somehow hurt her position at her old job? She drew in a breath as a sudden case of nerves overwhelmed her with doubt. As much as she loved the adventurous nature of her summer job, was she being practical?

She found herself hoping to go back to her old routine as soon as possible. Why did she think she could make a big change in her life? Fulfill a life-long dream as a musician. That wasn't her.

Dana swung the car toward the cottages and stopped in front of number six. After unloading her luggage, she dragged it all into her unit and dropped it on the bed. The cottage was small but very neat. A tiny kitchen with a table for two was at the front, a bed and dresser in the middle, then a seating area with loveseat and coffee table. A stone fireplace took over one wall. Her teeth chattered and a hot shower beckoned.

She showered and changed into jeans and a tee shirt and slipped on a lightweight hooded sweatshirt, leaving it unzipped. Grabbing her room key and stuffing it in her sweatshirt pocket, she gave her unpacked suitcases a weary look as she left her cottage.

When she tried Jack's door and got no answer, she accepted the grim fact that harp practice would have to wait until after the meeting that evening. The castle loomed in front of her and begged exploration. A drive into town for groceries would wait. How could she pass up scouting the grounds of a five-hundred-year-old monument? Closed or not, she had to take a closer look. She had all afternoon to shop and unpack. As she climbed the hill toward the castle, she admired how the dark stone structure rose well above the trees and at each corner were tower-like turrets. The view from the top must be amazing.

After working in a security company for thirteen years, force of habit had her scanning the castle walls for security cameras or spotlights. No cameras, minimal lighting, no motion sensors. She hoped the park had a better system in place inside, considering the castle was supposed to have fifteenth- and sixteenth-century furnishings.

Why did the castle have to be closed today? Just her luck. She walked up the drawbridge and tried the door and found it locked. Crap. Maybe it wasn't so easy to break into a castle.

Walking around the building, she ran her hand along the rough stone. Five hundred years old. She tried to imagine what it would've been like to live here centuries ago. The sophisticated lords and ladies must have had many lavish feasts and celebrations. And all summer she would be entertaining in this beautiful, historical place. A dream come true. She couldn't contain her smile.

She hadn't practiced in over two weeks since she'd shipped her harp. Even though the audiences for the dinner shows would be small, her stomach knotted as if she was about to perform at a huge symphony hall.

Three-quarters around the building, she discovered a small alcove and a wooden service door at the end of the narrow walkway. Dana tugged on the metal door latch and it opened. She shook her head. Very poor security. She should mention this to Jack and make some recommendations while she was here.

A narrow curved stairway led up. She preferred to learn the layout of the place before she started work, since the first show would be in a couple of days. One flight up opened onto a great hall. A few tapestries hung on the walls between giant windows and heavy dark chairs and one table nearly took up the entire room. They'd need more tables to seat guests. There must be another room.

Dana crossed the hall to another doorway that led to a different stairway and was about to climb, when she saw a flickering glow from the darkness below. Fire? Could the castle be on fire? Wiring or the furnishings could be. She trotted down the circular stone stairs.

Darkness crept in around her except for the golden, flickering light from the basement. Walking through another doorway, she thought she heard voices but she wasn't sure. The hairs on the back of her neck stood up.

As she rounded a stone partition, the room brightened. Flames flickered within a half dozen wrought-iron sconces; a fire burned in a small stone fireplace. The room smelled of sweet burning wood and damp stone. At the far wall two people hovered in shadows. Dana remained in her circle of darkness at the bottom of the stairs, unable to tear her gaze away from the frightening sight.

A naked woman, suspended from the ceiling, was bound with straps. Her wrists and ankles secured and spread wide in a V shape. Torn between wanting to rush over to rescue her, or run out and call for help, Dana froze. She couldn't move or speak.

A narrow hammock cradled and supported the woman's back and bottom. Her pussy and anus lay open wide, and metal clamps were attached to her nipples. Dana winced at the distended tips protruding from the tight clamps. The woman also wore a blindfold. The other person, a male, wore a hooded robe. His back faced Dana.

A rush of heat, then cold crept through her. Wrapping her arms around her waist, her first instinct was to escape and call for help. Then she stepped back and searched for a weapon, planning to do some damage to the guy if the woman needed help. Instead, Dana froze at the bottom of the stairs. Attacking this man was not a good idea if the woman was a willing participant. She would watch long enough to make sure the woman was okay.

There were people who got into this kinky stuff. Why would this woman allow this man to do these things? "More, slave?" the man in the robe asked the woman.

The woman nodded. "Yes, Master, if it pleases you." His fingers stroked the narrow thatch of dark hair between her legs, avoiding the glistening folds of her pussy. The woman squirmed and tried lifting her hips.

Dana managed to breathe in teaspoon-sized portions of air. People did this for fun? It didn't look like fun. Was the woman in trouble? Should she stop this? Go for help? Move, dammit.

"You want me to touch your clit, don't you?"

The woman whimpered and arched her back. "Yes, Sir."

"But I hadn't given you permission to move." He continued to tease her, his fingers trailing along her inner thighs, across her ass and back to the thatch of hair.

The woman moaned in pleasure. "No, Sir. You didn't. I forgot."

His hand moved to her breasts and adjusted the nipple clamps until she let out a little yelp and sharp intake of breath. "I'll have to punish you for forgetting."

"Yes, Sir."

He swung a flogger in the air several times. The woman's chest rose and fell quickly as if anticipating the blows that would come. Dana held her breath. The robed man struck her ass and she cried out and jerked against her bindings. Her feet pointed and her legs tried to spread wider.

"Yes, Master, again. Please."

Biting her lip, Dana clamped a hand over her mouth. Good lord, the woman enjoyed this.

"Not just yet. You're being an insolent slave today." He chuckled as the flogger swatted her bottom and the underside of her thighs.

Dana's blood chilled with the sharp crack of leather hitting the woman's bare skin. As he hit her again and again, the woman slumped in her restraints, her head hung to one side. He approached her and brushed her long dark hair from her face and kissed her forehead tenderly. Whimpering, the woman leaned into the kiss. Dana stared at the couple shamelessly. She should leave quietly but couldn't pull herself away.

"Good," he said. "You ready for more?"

The woman nodded and leaned into his hand. He walked over to the wall and pulled an object out of a tote bag then came back to the woman.

"You remember the safe signals with a gag?"

"Yes, Master. Three quick grunts or open and close my hands."

"Yes." He bent down to kiss her. "Now open." A ball gag was secured in her mouth. He tied the straps around the back of her head. Now the woman couldn't scream if she needed to.

Dana couldn't shout or run. Should she trust this man or do something?

"You're such a pain slut, my love." The man stroked her hair then he swung the flogger in a circle. Turning to the side, the man faced Dana. His robe gaped open, and he was naked underneath. His hard cock jutted out from the draped fabric. "I think you like pain as much as coming."

The woman made a mewling sound as she nodded.

"You want to come, don't you?" His hand slipped between her legs, then he plunged a finger inside her.

She nodded and moaned, trying to raise her hips.

"No, stay," he ordered, pulling his hand away. He then swung the flogger and swatted straight across her breasts.

The woman gave a yelp as much as she could with a gag in her mouth.

Dana bit her lip as heat flowed through her followed by a throbbing in her pussy. Lord, she was wet and getting turned on by this. The man lapped at the woman's clamped nipples, then took a swollen tip between his teeth. The woman jerked against her restraints. "Too painful?" he asked.

She shook her head and arched her back, offering her breasts to him. He bit harder this time and the woman cried out beneath the gag. Dana's nipples hardened too and her pussy was sopping. How could the woman stand that kind of torture and appear to beg for more?

"Are you ready to be fucked?" he asked as his hand dipped down to her slit.

She nodded, writhing in her restraints.

"I'm going to fuck you, but I want to taste you first."

The woman let out a groan and looked at her right hand. She had her pinky finger extended. He looked up. "You're signaling you're on the edge?"

She nodded.

"Good. I'll go slowly." He cracked the flogger in the air. The sound made the woman and Dana jump. "But don't come until I give you permission. I still wish to taste you so you must remain in control."

The woman nodded slightly and whimpered. Stroking her breasts, the man then moved his hand lower, circling her pussy. His mouth positioned between her legs and Dana could see he blew across her clit and labia. The woman groaned. Dana held her hand over her mouth.

Obviously, these were lovers, strange as it was, and she needed to get out of there before they saw her. Slowly, she took a step back and another, but somehow managed to trip over her own feet in the darkness. Stumbling, she fell back against the wall. The movement and noise caught the man's attention. He jerked his head toward Dana and gave her a narrowed look.

End of preview for Edge of Passion, Book 2.

Preview
Tattoo Witch

CHAPTER ONE

"Sam, stop. People will see us." Anita shoved his chest.

"It was only a kiss," Sam teased.

"Yeah, sure. You grabbed my breasts." She rushed past him, heading toward the beach that overlooked the bay of Ocean City, Maryland. Moonlight glistened on the water and an offshore breeze thrashed at the palm fronds. Maybe he was pushing too hard. This vacation was supposed to stir up a little excitement in their life, especially their sex life. He didn't need to pressure her.

His girlfriend stood at the shoreline, her arms wrapped tightly around her waist. She swayed to the reggae music playing in the background. Annoyed, but not angry. A year together and he still couldn't keep his eyes or hands off her. The wind whipped strands of her long, brown hair against high cheekbones, a petite nose and dimpled chin. Anita always complained that her jawline was too angular, but Sam said it gave her a sexy, brainy look. He was pretty certain she wore the tight skirt for him. She knew it was his favorite. When they first met, he was entranced by her eyes, not her curvy ass. Behind that gaze, he'd sensed an intelligent, kind and affectionate person. Then he'd noticed her hot ass. Many times she flashed those sultry, hazel eyes, trying to work him around her finger. He even played along on occasion.

"Ouch!" Anita hopped on one foot as she kicked off her shoe. "I stepped on a shell or something."

"Hold onto me." Sam brushed off her sandal and foot, then slipped the sandal back on. "Better?"

She nodded. Hooking her arms around his neck, she kissed him. Her low–cut tank offered a glimpse of cleavage.

Most of the clientele from Seacrets, the outdoor bar, restaurant and nightclub, were dancing near the band or seated at tables eating dinner. No one was by the beach area. "I thought it'd be romantic here," he explained, trying to keep his voice light as he stared out over the water.

Several round floats, the size of small mattresses, bobbed in the water. Unlike daytime, the beachside bar was closed. The boat dock, deserted. She gave him that don't-bull-shit-me look. He knew what that meant. They'd been together long enough for him to know all her expressions and moods. "You wanted to fool around," she said.

"What's wrong with that?"

She frowned, then finally smiled and slipped her arm around him, giving in a little. "Nothing. But I don't care to get groped in public."

"I didn't grope you," he argued.

"You grabbed my breasts."

"I was checking to see if you wore a bra tonight."

"Right." She huffed. "I always wear a bra."

"I know, just fantasizing."

She leaned into him. "I love fooling around with you. We can fool around when we get back to the hotel."

If he kept arguing, he wouldn't get any tonight. "Okay. Ready for a drink?"

"Shhhh." Anita's eyes widened and gripped his arm.

Sam felt his cock grow hard. "Change your mind?"

"No, be quiet. Look, on the raft."

"Where?"

"By the boat dock. The last one in the back row," she whispered.

Lights from the dock shone on a naked couple lying on one of the rafts and fucking like porn stars. "Cool. At least someone's getting lucky."

Anita punched him in the arm...hard.

"Ow."

"Let's go," she whispered.

"No, let's watch. If we leave now, they'll know we saw them." A lame excuse, but the only one he could come up with at the moment.

"So? They obviously don't care." Anita strained for a closer look. "What's he wearing? Does he have a shirt on?"

Sam tried to make out the man who was pumping his cock into his woman and somehow managing to keep from tipping the raft over. "No, I think he has tattoos, a lot of them. He's got great balance. With all that thrusting how does he manage not to flip the raft?"

"It is pretty hot to watch," Anita said with a raspy voice.

"Yeah." Was she getting turned on? How cool would that be? With his hand on her waist, Sam slid upward and grazed the underside of her breast. He was rewarded with her sharp intake of breath. Encouraged, he let his hand slide down and underneath her shirt. This time when he grasped her breast, she didn't protest. Hallelujah.

"Feels good," she whispered, leaning into him. Her full lips glistened, begging to be kissed. He took the chance and lowered his mouth to her lips. She pressed a hand to his chest. "Stop. Look, they've finished anyway." The couple had climbed up on the boat dock and got dressed.

Disappointed, Sam took his hand out from under Anita's shirt. His cock was still freaking hard.

"I'm ready for that drink," she said.

"Right," he muttered.

They ordered drinks from an outside bar that was built to look like an old shipwrecked boat. Sam took a swig from his beer and Anita sipped on her rum punch. "There they are." He tilted his head as the exhibitionists approached the bar. The woman had on a low-cut top that showed off a decent set of breasts and several tats on her arms, shoulders and chest. He wondered how far down the ink went. No doubt the design circled each breast. His cock came to life again. Hey, he was a guy after all.

Her short red hair was damp from their evening swim. Her man was well built, about the same height as Sam, with sandy colored hair that came down past his shoulders. He wore a black Harley tee with the sleeves cut out. Both arms were covered in tats. His neck had a coiled snake or a dragon design. The tattooed man and woman sat next to Sam and Anita. Sam noticed the wedding bands.

Anita vigorously stirred the bottom of her drink while sucking on the straw and slurping the last of the frozen concoction.

"I think your lady is ready for another drink," tattooed guy said with a friendly tone. "Mind if my wife and I buy you two a drink?"

Anita stopped slurping and gave Sam a warning look. He loved his girlfriend dearly, but wished she wasn't quite so conservative. This couple was just being friendly. But why did they decide to sit next to him and Anita?

Stop assuming the worst. Sam Quinn was used to expecting the worst in people—a side effect from working airport security. Terrorists at Seacrets were likely a low-risk concern. Perhaps this couple did have ulterior motives, like wife swapping. That wasn't exactly Sam's kink, but it didn't mean he couldn't have some fun chatting with them. "A drink? That's nice of you to offer," Sam said. "You don't have to—"

"It's our pleasure," the woman added. "I'm Rene and this is my husband, Perry. We're from Baltimore." She rested her hands on the bar. On the back of Rene's hand was a detailed rose tat. It looked 3D. Ink designs covered Perry's hands too.

Sam introduced himself and Anita. Anita gave him a kick. He was going to get hell later, but the intricate detail of Rene's tattoo was mesmerizing.

"Have you tried Swamp Water?" Perry asked Anita.

She looked confused.

"They're good. They're coconut rum, pineapple juice and Curaçao. Try one," Rene said as she waved to the bartender and ordered two and a couple beers.

"We were about to leave, right Sam?" Anita shot him a look.

"Oh, you can hang for a drink," Rene said. "It's still early."

Anita scowled at her murky green drink when it arrived but didn't argue with Rene. Taking a sip, she smiled. "Mmmm. It is good."

"What kind of work do you do, Sam?" Perry asked.

"TSA agent."

"Interesting." Perry locked his gaze with him. Red flags waved in the back of Sam's mind.

As a TSA agent, Sam had an uncanny gift of reading people's eyes, expressions and body language. Something in Perry's gaze alarmed him. If someone had looked at him like that while going through his TSA check point, he would give them a pat down. What were his eyes telling him? A warning? Fear? A challenge or threat? Sam couldn't figure it out. Something wasn't right about these two. Or maybe he needed this vacation more than he thought.

"I've been admiring your tattoos," Sam said as he watched their expressions. "Excellent work. It must've taken a long time to have those done. Were they all by the same artist?"

Perry and Rene exchanged a look. "Yes, she's local," Perry said. "On the boardwalk."

"I don't remember a tattoo parlor and we come here often." Anita had sucked down half her drink. "What do you have on your neck?" she asked Perry.

Perry got up and sat on the stool next to her. Turning his head to the side, he elongated his neck, offering Anita a better view. "What would you call it?"

"It's a dragon. A magnificent dragon. Look at all the colors." While Perry pointed out his various tattoos, Rene showed the vine of roses coiling up her arm.

"Do the tats have specific meanings or stories?" Sam asked. "They're very detailed."

She laughed out loud. "Sort of."

He noticed a shadow of sadness drift across Rene's face. Anita was oblivious to his conversation. The designs on the man's forearms enthralled her. She was literally staring. Fuck.

"Do you think tattoos are sexy?" Rene asked seductively.

"I guess." He forced himself not to look at her deep cleavage and the tats that decorated her skin there. Man, he needed to take Anita back to the hotel and fuck her brains out before she got wasted on Swamp Water.

"How about mine?" Rene ran her hands over her arms, then stroked the tops of her breasts.

"Yes, I'd say so," Sam replied. Holy shit, she was flirting with him. "There." Rene eased the sleeve of Sam's tee shirt up over his shoulder. "You have nice biceps and shoulders. The perfect place for tats." Her fingernail drew imaginary designs on his arm.

He studied her with the narrowed gaze he reserved for troublemakers at the airport and added a cocky smile. "Think so?"

"Yes," she breathed, leaning closer. "Men also look hot with tats on their calves and thighs. Her hand dropped to his knee, just below his cargo shorts. Would she slide those up too? His cock stirred. How much had she drunk?

Anita laughed. Sam glanced at Perry flexing his arm, making a scorpion tat appear to crawl. His girlfriend was amused.

"Have you ever thought about getting a tat?" Rene asked Sam with a sultry, teasing tone. "Or maybe you have one hidden?" She removed her hand from his knee. Sam released his breath. "No. I've thought about getting one. But I don't have any." Damn, it was getting warm. Was Rene coming on to him with her husband right there? He glanced back at Anita again. She was having another Swamp Water. Terrific.

"You should get one. You and your lady," Rene said. "We get ours at Sinful Designs on the boardwalk. They do the best work."

Ah, now he got it. "I suppose you two work there? Or own the business."

She laughed. "You think we're trying to drum up sales?"

Sam nodded.

"No, nothing like that. But there is something special about Sinful Designs that you won't find at any other tattoo parlor."

"Is that right?" Sam called over the bartender and ordered another beer and a drink for Rene. "Don't take this the wrong way but are you two hitting on us?"

"Not exactly," Perry said, looking up from his show-and-tell for Anita. "We saw you watching us earlier—"

"And you thought we'd like to hook up with you two," Sam finished the sentence, sounding slightly annoyed but intrigued.

"That's not it," Rene said. "But I bet you wished you were out there having the most amazing sex with Anita. Am I right?"

"Sure," Sam said.

Anita smiled nervously, then sipped more of her drink.

"What if I told you there was a way to increase your sexual enjoyment by at least ten times, be more adventurous, have longer hard-ons, and multiple orgasms?" Rene looked at Anita. "Anita, wouldn't you love to have multiple orgasms whenever you willed them to happen?"

Anita rolled her eyes. "I have orgasms."

"Four or five in one night, without being touched?"

"I'd say you're full of shit," Anita said.

Sam nearly choked on his beer. Anita Brooke never swore in front of strangers. She was getting drunk. Damn, he wasn't getting any tonight.

"Do you believe in magic, the supernatural?"

"I try to keep an open mind." Sam didn't want to discount anything. But more than that, he wanted to see where this was going.

"Try one of these tattoos at Sinful Designs. Just one. I promise you won't be disappointed." Rene paused. "Don't be surprised if you go back for more like we did." Eyes wide, she glanced around the night club's grounds, looked over her shoulder, then forced a smile. There was no hiding that look of terror. Cold fear flashed across her eyes. What had her so afraid? She didn't look the type to scare easily. A shiver slid down Sam's spine.

"Sounds too good to be true," Sam said as he briefly fantasized a few possibilities—sex on the raft, sex with this couple, and a few positions Anita wasn't crazy about trying. His cock throbbed as his heart pounded in his chest. The woman didn't look like she was lying. Was business that bad that this tattoo parlor would think up this fantastical story to bring in a few customers?

Rene placed a hand on his arm. "Honest, Sam, we don't make out financially if you get a tattoo. We're just amazed by this woman. She's a witch you know. Her name is Cassandra."

"A witch?" Anita asked.

Rene smiled at Sam. "Trust me. You will have the most scorching sex you could ever imagine."

End of preview for Tattoo Witch, Book 3.